THE DESIGNS OF Love

JOYCE ARMINTROUT

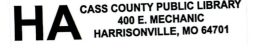

PAGE PUBLISHING, INC.
New York, NY

First originally published by Page Publishing, Inc. 2016

ISBN 978-1-68409-385-4 (Paperback)
ISBN 978-1-68409-386-1 (Digital)

Printed in the United States of America

CHAPTER ONE

*I*t was going to be very difficult to leave here, but after what had happened, how could she stay?

This ranch was the only home she had ever known. This room was her sanctuary since she could remember.

She loved sitting by the windows, watching the ever-changing Colorado scenery outside them. On the north was a towering mountain peak she had nicknamed Polly. Over the years, she had come to think of Polly as someone to whom she could tell her deepest, darkest secrets. Countless problems had been solved by using her friend, the mountain, as a sounding board.

The west window overlooked spacious rolling hills, a vista she could always count on to bring her tranquility. Quite often, she saw antelope mixed in with her father's Hereford cattle grazing on the lush prairie grasses.

The nearest town was Everett, and it was ten miles away, but she never felt isolated. It was only about seventy-five miles to Denver if she ever felt the need to do some serious shopping.

She really had no one to go to for advice since her mother's death five years earlier. Her father, concerned about his own mortality, had been far too busy preparing her older brother to take over the operation of the ranch businesses to have time to pay any attention to his teenage daughter and her problems.

The few times she attempted to talk with him about something that was important to her, he had referred her to their housekeeper.

Agnes Barry was a nice enough person, but she was not much help when it came to giving helpful advice to a teenager.

The housekeeper's daughter Sheryl had spent her summer vacations at the ranch while she was in college. Despite the four-year difference in age, the two girls had become good friends. Sheryl listened to Abby's problems and offered advice when asked. Some of it was actually quite helpful, but it wasn't the same as having a mother to talk with whenever she felt the need for a little guidance.

She wrote Sheryl to tell her about the barbecue party at Gerald and Katherine Tracy's and their son Tyler's surprise announcement of his engagement to Jennifer Winslow, a girl he had only known for six weeks, for gosh sakes! Sheryl understood how Abby felt and offered to let the unhappy girl move in with her until they could figure out what she should do next.

She dreaded telling her father about her decision to leave the ranch because she was sure he would be dead set against it.

Earlier in the day, she had discussed with her brother, Doug, her plans to leave, and he agreed it might be better for her if she did get away, at least for a little while. He was sure she would get over her hurt and would want to move back home within a few weeks.

After dinner that evening, she asked to speak privately with her father so she could explain her plans to him and attempt to get his approval of her moving in with Sheryl.

"It's a waste of time for you to move away from here, Abby. You will want to move back when you get married." Her father then laid out his plans for her. "Hank Spenser told me just last week that Witt has hopes of marrying you one day. We discussed the situation and decided that when the time comes, he will give you both a section of land situated between this ranch and his as a wedding present and I will build you a house. I already have the perfect location for it picked out. You're just going to love it! It has a beautiful view."

"But I don't want to marry Witt! I'm not in love with him!" she objected, more than a little surprised at her father's plan. All this time, she thought he had been ignoring her. "I'm not just a part of this ranch, Dad! You can't run my life like you do everything else around here. It's time for me to leave here and make my own way for

4

a while. Sheryl has offered to share her apartment in Centerview with me until I decide what I want to do. I have the monthly stipend from Mother's estate to tide me over until I can find a job," she pleaded with her dad.

"I've never been anywhere or done anything! I need to get a job and support myself, at least for a little while. Maybe I can take some night classes to learn to do something. Sheryl will look after me and help me find a job. She works at a department store in a mall, so maybe I can find something there. I'm not saying I will be gone forever. I love this house, and I've been very happy here on the ranch. I could never forget my roots." She reasoned with her father. "I have to do this for myself, Dad. Please try to understand."

"You are so much like your mother." He looked intently at her for a long moment and then continued, "You have an independent streak just like she did. I think that's what first attracted me to her. We were so different that her family thought she was making a terrible mistake when she married me. I think that difference was what made our marriage work so well. She wouldn't let me get away with anything, and I loved her for that. When she left us, I felt like the best part of me went with her." He sighed deeply, lost in his memories for the moment, and then added, "I may not like it, but I have a feeling that ultimately you will do what you think is best for you. I think I understand how you feel and why you want to leave just now. Tyler Tracy's little announcement last week must have hit you pretty hard."

"But how do you know about my feelings for Tyler? I have never mentioned a word about it to you or Doug." Abby was shocked at that revelation.

"Oh, I've known for quite a while that you thought you were in love with the boy. I suspected it was a teenage crush and hoped it would blow over in due time," he explained, paused a moment, took a deep breath, and then continued, "I'm not the insensitive bum, I'm sure you sometimes think I am. I can and do observe things that are going on around me. I don't always show it, but I do care about your feelings. So if you must go, do so with my blessing. Just come home and visit your old dad once in a while and know that you will always have a home here if you ever feel the need for it. Now, come give me a hug and then go make your arrangements with Sheryl."

"Dad, you never cease to amaze me. All these years I thought you didn't know I was alive. Now I find out you have been paying attention all along—just not in the way I expected." Abby gave her dad an extra hug before letting him go.

"Never doubt that I love you, Daughter. I'm just not very good at showing it. That was always your mother's department. Remember, I will always want what's best for you even if I sometimes don't exactly agree with your choices."

Layton Andrews sighed deeply as he watched his daughter leave the room to take her first steps as an independent woman. This was certainly one of those times when he didn't agree with her plans, but it was time for him to let her go so she could do what she felt she needed to.

***

The first thing Abby did was to call Sheryl to confirm that she could move in with her. She knew Sheryl had been looking for a roommate and probably needed the extra income, so she insisted she be allowed to split the expenses with Sheryl while she lived there. Sheryl readily accepted the arrangement, and they agreed the move would be made the next Sunday.

Even though she could have made the move by herself, with Sheryl's help, Abby enlisted both her dad and brother to help her because she thought they might feel better if they could see something of the area where she would be living.

"Are you absolutely sure you want to do this?" Her dad gave her one last chance to change her mind before he put her luggage in the Land Rover.

"No, I don't really want to, but it's something I have to do, for me." Standing on tiptoe, she gave her father a peck on the cheek. "Thank you for understanding and letting me go."

"If you must go through with this, then let's get on the road." Lay sighed as he picked up one of her bags. He was going to miss that girl more than he cared to admit.

After about an hour's drive, they pulled up in front of the three-story buff brick building where Sheryl lived in an apartment on the top floor.

The elevator was temporarily out of service, so Abby was grateful to have extra help carrying her personal belongings up the two flights of stairs.

Sheryl invited the men to have some iced tea and cool off before they started back.

"It's been a while since I've seen you, Sheryl. How have you been?" Doug opened the conversation while making himself comfortable in a chair near where Sheryl was seated.

"I'm getting along just fine. I guess it's probably been at least a couple of years since the last time I saw you. The last few times I was there to see Mother, you were away for one reason or another," Sheryl answered.

"If I remember right, I was up in Oregon, looking at a new bull for the ranch one time. I think once I was on a fishing trip. Don't remember where I was the other times. On some ranch business probably," Doug explained.

"Traveling like that must be exciting. Do you do it very often?" Sheryl asked.

"Oh, just once in a while, not really that often. Dad usually goes on those buying trips." Doug continued, "Let me know the next time you come home to see your mother, and I will try to be there to show you around the place. We've made a few changes in the last couple of years."

"I'll do that," Sheryl promised.

"I get over here to Centerview fairly often. The next time I'm in town, I would like to take the both of you out to dinner if it's okay with you," Doug suggested.

"That would be fine with me." Sheryl was beginning to find Doug interesting.

"Well, son, we had better be heading home. We need to get those steers sorted so they will be ready to load when the trucks get there in the morning." The elder Andrews interrupted the conversation, anxious to return to the ranch and the work that was waiting for them.

"I guess you are right, Dad." Doug was enjoying the conversation. He had known Sheryl since her mother had become their housekeeper five years earlier, but this was the first time he had sat down and really had a conversation with her. He found her intriguing, so he intended to get to know her a little better. Having his sister as her roommate might work out very well. He intended to visit Abby as often as he had time.

"Mr. Andrews, it was nice to see you again. Doug, I will look forward to seeing you soon." Sheryl was sorry to see Doug leave.

"It was nice to visit with you also, Sheryl. Take good care of my little girl." Lay bid her good-bye as he walked to the door, anxious to be on his way.

"It was really good to see you again, Sheryl, and I will visit you soon, I promise." Doug hated to cut the visit short, but duty called, and the work had to be done.

Abby walked the men to their car to say her good-byes. She hugged them both and promised she would be careful of strangers and call home often.

By the time Abby returned to the apartment, Sheryl had carried most of her cases into what was to be her bedroom.

"I'm really glad you came. Let's get you settled, and then we'll see if we can come up with a plan to keep you here, at least until you are ready to move on." Sheryl opened one of the suitcases and began hanging some of Abby's clothes in the closet while Abby busied herself filling the chest drawers with her personal things.

"It's good to be here. I'm thankful you asked me to move in with you. I don't know what I would have done if I had to stay home and see Tyler with that Jennifer every time I turned around," Abby answered, truly grateful that Sheryl had given her a means of escape.

"Are you still into designing your own clothes?" Sheryl asked as the two girls, finished with the business of unpacking, set about preparing their evening meal.

"Yes, I still design and make them." Abby wondered at the question.

"There's a little tailor shop at the mall near the store where I work. I saw a Help Wanted sign in the window yesterday. Tomorrow is my day off, so let's go over there and see what kind of help they need. I understand they make custom clothing and do tailoring, so maybe it's something you would be interested in."

"It would be great if I can get a job near here and so soon." Maybe things would work out for her after all.

***

"Hi, I'm Abby Andrews, and I came in to inquire as to what kind of help you need."

"Hello. I'm Georgia Tabor. We need someone to design special-order garments for customers. I can do the sewing, but I need someone to draw up the designs and patterns. Do you have a portfolio that I can look at?"

"No, I'm sorry I don't. I have been designing clothes for myself for a number of years, but this is the first time I have applied for a job doing that." Abby's heart fell. She hadn't thought about bringing any of her designs with her.

"I've seen her work, Mrs. Tabor. I'm sure you won't be disappointed," Sheryl added.

"Did you make the outfit you have on?" Mrs. Tabor looked critically at Abby's three-piece suit.

"Yes. It's one I designed and made." Abby did a pirouette to show the outfit off.

"It's very nice." The older woman looked at Abby for a moment, then finished, "I think I will take a chance on you. I'll need to talk to my son before I can make it permanent. He's away on a trip right now, but I don't imagine he will have any objections. Would it be possible for you start in the morning?"

"Absolutely! Thank you, Mrs. Tabor. What time do you want me to come in?" Abby was elated to find work so soon.

"Come in at eight. We open at nine, but you will need to fill out some forms before you start. We're not very formal around here, so please call me Georgia."

"It'll be good to have you here, Abby." Georgia welcomed Abby with a warm handshake.

"That worked out well," a very relieved Abby said as they walked to the car.

"Lunch is on me. You pick the place." Sheryl suggested.

"I guess I had better think about getting a car, sometime soon." It was something Abby hadn't thought about. At home, she just used one of the ranch vehicles, but she couldn't rely on Sheryl to take her every place she needed to go.

"I'll drive you over early in the morning. The rest of the time you are welcome to ride with me. It sounds as though we will be pretty much on the same schedule. There is always the bus or a taxi if you really need to go somewhere. If you want to wait until you get a few paychecks before you look for a car, it's all right. I don't think there needs to be any rush," Sheryl offered.

"Doug did say he would be by to see us once in a while. Maybe he will help me find a good used one. When I'm ready to get one, I'll call him to see when he can take time to help me look." She would feel better if a man were there to help her find the right car for her. Probably, she would get a better deal if her brother went with her.

***

Abby quickly adapted to her new position. She had a client almost as soon as the store opened.

Katherine Parker needed a special dress for a company party, and she had very specific ideas as to how it should look. After a couple of tries, she decided on a design Abby drew, with a couple of minor alterations. Abby drew up a pattern, and when the fabric came in, Georgia set about making it. In less than two weeks, the customer left with a truly breathtaking one-of-a-kind creation.

The very next day, Eleanor Davis came into the shop on the recommendation of Mrs. Parker.

Her daughter's wedding was in ten days, and she was in a panic. Her tailor had become ill, so he would not be able to provide her with the dress she had ordered. Abby drew up a couple of sketches for her to look at. After a brief discussion, they decided to combine the two designs and came up with a unique style that pleased everyone.

With both Abby and Georgia working on the project, they finished the creation three days before the wedding.

One morning, while she was with a client, Abby noticed a very good-looking young man enter the shop and go directly to Georgia's office. She assumed him to be the son.

As soon as Abby was free, Georgia confirmed that thought.

"Abby, I would like you to meet my son, Allen." Georgia made the introduction.

"Hello, Allen. It's nice to meet you." Abby extended her hand.

"It's a pleasure to make your acquaintance, Abby." Allen took her hand and held onto it until she withdrew. "It's nearly time for lunch, so why don't you let me take you somewhere to eat while we get to know each other?"

"You have an appointment at one fifteen, Abby, so be sure to be back by then." Georgia reminded the both of them not to take too long.

"Don't worry, Mother. I will have her back in plenty of time," Allen assured his mother as he took Abby's arm to escort her out of the shop.

"Mother tells me this is your very first job and that you just recently moved to town." Allen opened the conversation as they waited for their lunch.

"Yes. I've designed and made my own clothes for a good bit of my life, but this is the first time I've ever actually tried to do it professionally," she admitted.

"From what Mother says, you apparently are pretty good at it," he commented, peering intently at the lovely girl across the table from him.

11

"It's easy to work at something you love. I am very fortunate to be able to do that." Abby was a little uncomfortable to be under such close scrutiny by her lunch companion.

"Where did you live?" Allen asked.

"I was born and raised about sixty miles northwest of here, on a ranch."

"That's lonely country out there. What did you do for entertainment?" Allen questioned her while they ate their salad.

"The area isn't very populated, but I had friends and a lot of activities to keep me busy." Abby hastened to assure him she had been very happy on the ranch.

"How far was the nearest town?" He kept her talking so he could gauge his approach to her. So far, he figured her to be a simple country girl.

"Everett is ten miles away. Our nearest neighbor lives five miles from my family home." She felt a quick pang of loneliness as she thought about home.

"Do you have a boyfriend?"

"No." She really didn't want to talk to him about that.

"I will have to take care of that." He smiled at her as he reached across the table and squeezed her hand confidently.

"I'm really not interested in having any sort of relationship right now. I just want to concentrate on my job for a while." She tried to discourage any plans he might be making for her.

"Oh, I will make sure you have plenty of time for your little job. I just want us to have a little fun when you are not working." He was sure she would succumb to his charms. They had rarely failed him before, so why would he have any trouble with this naive kid just off the farm?

"I think we should get back to work." She had a bad feeling about Allen. He could cause her a lot of trouble if she upset him. "We're going to be late."

"Okay, for now. We can talk more later." He looked at his watch and signaled the waiter to bring their check.

"See, Mother, I almost got her back on time," he greeted Georgia upon their arrival back at the shop.

"I was beginning to wonder. Mrs. Hayden came in early, Abby. I have her looking at some of the fabric sample books until you returned."

"I'm so sorry, Georgia. I won't let this happen again, I promise," Abby apologized for being late. "Time just got away from me."

"No harm done. It's easy for time to slip by when you are enjoying yourself." Georgia accepted Abby's apology.

***

The days flew by for Abby. Most of the time, she was kept busy with clients. The only fly in the ointment was Allen. So far, she had been able to put off his advances, but he was getting more and more insistent that she go out with him.

She could feel his eyes on her most of the time when she was with clients. She was running out of excuses as to why she couldn't go out with him. She was invariably polite with him because she didn't want to hurt Georgia's feelings or upset him, but the truth of the matter was that she just plain didn't feel comfortable around Allen.

"Let's go out to eat somewhere tonight and then take in a movie." He couldn't understand her reluctance to go out with him. "You don't have to work tomorrow, so it won't hurt if we are late getting home."

"I'm sorry, Allen. I'm just getting over a big disappointment with someone, and I'm not ready to start anything up just yet." She decided to try a little straight talk. Maybe that would help.

"You had a boyfriend? Why am I just now hearing about this?" He didn't for one minute believe her!

"I really didn't feel up to discussing it." That part was true. She didn't want to talk about Tyler. "I'm sorry I didn't tell you sooner, but I really am trying to forget that part of my life. I moved here so I could make a clean break from old memories."

"When do you think you are going to be over him? I could help you forget him, if you would let me." That might explain why she refused all of his advances. Maybe he shouldn't give up just yet in case she was telling him the truth. He was going to have to think about this.

"I don't know how long it will take to get over him, but I am just not interested in you that way. I would prefer to keep our relationship strictly business. I'm sorry, Allen, but that's the way I feel." She hoped he would understand. "It's time for me to go meet my ride. I'll see you Monday morning."

She didn't give him time to answer because she hoped if he took a little time to think about what she had said, just maybe he would be a little more sympathetic to her situation.

Allen was waiting for Abby on Monday morning, and Georgia was nowhere to be seen.

"How was your weekend, Abby?" He asked.

"It was okay." She wondered at the question and his presence.

Allen generally didn't arrive at the shop until midmorning, so she knew something was up.

"I've been thinking about your qualifications for this job. I really think we need someone with a little more experience for a position such as this." He got to the point quickly. "I made some inquiries over the weekend, and I think I have found someone who meets our requirements. I've made out your last check. We will pay you for the whole week in lieu of notice. Your replacement will be here tomorrow, so I'm sure you understand why you can't stay." He finished with smirk as he dropped Abby's check on the desk in front of her.

Abby gathered her personal items as quickly as possible. She didn't want to let Allen know how upset she was. This was the last thing she expected. As far as she knew, Georgia had been happy with her work. Where was Georgia? She was always there early to unlock the shop and stayed after Abby left. She wondered who made the decision to let her go, but she guessed it didn't matter because either way she was out of a job.

After stopping to tell Sheryl what happened, she took a cab home to lick her wounds and think about what she was going to do next.

She didn't want to tell Doug or her dad because they probably would want her to come home, and she couldn't do that. Maybe Sheryl would have an idea by the time she got home.

Sheryl was incensed that Allen would try to pull something that underhanded on her friend.

"He didn't replace you because he wanted someone with experience! He fired you because you wouldn't play ball with him! He just used the experience excuse so maybe you wouldn't sue him for sexual harassment. I think you should go ahead and sue him anyway!" Sheryl urged Abby to at least think about taking action against Allen. "You can't let him get away with something like that! I'll guarantee you this is not the first time he's pulled that stunt!"

Abby spent the next few days going over the want ads. She found a few openings she probably would have been suited for, but she really wanted to try to find something in the fashion industry.

One day Sheryl came home with a bit of hopeful news for her.

She had discussed what had happened to Abby and her job with her supervisor. Mrs. Jones was not at all surprised by the situation. She told Sheryl she had heard rumors about similar things happening before at Tabor's. She really didn't think Georgia knew anything about what her son was doing. The two women occasionally had lunch together, and Georgia had bemoaned the fact that she was having trouble keeping help. She said that they all quit within two or three weeks after starting to work. She just didn't understand what was causing them to leave for no apparent reason.

"I still think you should sue the bum! I bet we could find some of those other girls to corroborate your story." Sheryl was still upset for Abby. "But that's not the news I have for you," Sheryl continued, offering to help. "Mrs. Jones has a sister who is getting ready to open a small dress shop. She is going to sell a few ready-made dresses, but she really wants to do custom-made clothing, and she is looking for a designer to work there. She won't be able to pay very much until she gets on her feet, but maybe you can work out something in lieu of salary. If you think you might be interested, I will see if I can get an interview set up for you."

"Of course, I'm interested! I will be happy to work cheap if it means I will be doing what I love. Set up a meeting, and just tell me where and when!" Abby was ecstatic.

By noon the next day, Abby had an appointment, and by three o'clock, she was on her way to meet her prospective new boss.

The new shop was just a couple of blocks from where Sheryl worked, so they could still share a ride to work.

"Hello. I'm Abby Andrews." She approached a woman seated behind the counter.

"Hi, I'm Margaret Haley. It's really nice to meet you. My sister tells me you are interested in working as a clothing designer. She also told me you are just getting started and that you are pretty good at it. Is that true?" The woman rose to greet Abby.

"Well, I don't quite know how to respond to that." Abby appreciated the straightforward manner of Mrs. Haley but was a little embarrassed at her words. "I've designed and made my own clothes and for some of my friends for several years, and I do love doing it. I seem to have a knack for fitting the design to the person."

Margaret explained her situation to Abby. She had been thinking about her own shop for a long time and had recently decided it was now or never. There was enough money to get the business started and keep it afloat for a while, but that didn't leave much for hired help. She had a pretty good head for business and was an adequate seamstress, but she needed someone to design the garments and draw up the patterns.

She offered Abby a nominal salary plus 10 percent of the profits to start. Assuming the business became profitable, she would receive a fair salary increase, and perhaps something could be worked out for her to buy a small percentage of the business if she had an interest in doing that. They would discuss the details later if and when the business started to succeed.

Margaret asked Abby to start work on Monday morning.

She called her dad as soon as she got back to her apartment. He was surprised at her news of the new job because she had not told him about losing the old one. She glossed over the reason for the change of jobs, not wanting to give him a reason to worry about her.

Doug came on the line, while she was talking to her dad, to see if he could take her and Sheryl out to dinner on Saturday evening.

She told him she would check with Sheryl and call him back. She was looking forward to seeing her brother again, so she hoped Sheryl would be free.

Sheryl was happy to accept Doug's offer for dinner. She asked Abby to call him before he had a chance to change his mind.

Abby wanted to ask Doug if he had heard anything about Tyler and his engagement, but she held her tongue. Perhaps it would be better if she didn't know any of the details.

When Doug showed up on their doorstep on Saturday shortly after noon, he wasn't alone. Much to Abby's surprise, Witt was with him.

"Do you remember our neighbor Dewitt Spenser, Sheryl?" Doug asked as the two men entered the apartment.

"Of course! It's been a while, but if I'm not mistaken, we called you Witt, didn't we?" Sheryl offered a hand to welcome her guest.

"That's right. It's good to see you again, Sheryl." Witt accepted Sheryl's hand.

"I asked Witt to keep me company on the ride down here. Besides, it might be more fun if there are four of us." Doug grinned at his sister, knowing she was most probably upset with him for setting her up with Witt. But this would give him more time to concentrate on Sheryl.

Despite her misgivings, Abby enjoyed the afternoon thoroughly. She was surprised at what a good conversationalist Witt had become. Why had she never noticed it before?

Sheryl took the group to the aquarium before they went to her favorite restaurant for an early dinner so it wouldn't be too late when the guys had to head home. All too soon, it was time to for the men to leave. Doug hated to call it a day because he couldn't remember having a more pleasant time.

Sheryl hoped Doug would come back soon, and Abby decided she wouldn't mind if Witt came along with him because she had certainly enjoyed spending the afternoon with him.

As for the guys, they discussed maybe getting rooms at a nearby motel for the night the next time so they could spend more time with the girls.

***

Abby liked working with Margaret. In some ways, she reminded her of her mother. She was so easy to talk with that soon Abby found herself telling Margaret about Tyler and why she had decided to leave Everett and move to Centerview. It felt good to talk to someone beside Sheryl about her feelings for Tyler. She felt like Margaret understood why she was hurting.

Margaret told her about her daughter, Carolyn. She had graduated from a college in upstate New York, two years earlier with a degree in fashion design. Margaret had big plans for the two of them opening a dress shop together, but once Carolyn got a taste of life in New York City, she decided that was where she wanted to be. She had a good job with one of the top fashion firms in New York City. Margaret still had hopes for the two of them working together some day, but as long as her daughter was happy, she was satisfied the way things were for the time being.

The first client came in on the second day to have a dress made for her twenty-fifth wedding anniversary party. Sarah Perkins had no idea what she wanted, so Margaret first helped her pick out fabric and a color that suited her complexion, while Abby determined a style that was becoming for her shape and age. She had three designs for the lady to look at in short order. After much indecision, she finally decided on one of the drawings with a few minor adjustments.

Their second client turned out to be Mrs. Davis. Abby had designed a dress for her to wear to her daughter's wedding while she was at the Tabor dress shop in the mall. She had returned to Tabor's for a second dress but wasn't satisfied with any of the designs they provided. Someone told her there was a new dress shop opening up near where she lived, so she decided to try it. She was overjoyed when she saw Abby working there. The client knew pretty much what she wanted, and in short order, Abby had a design she was pleased with.

When Mrs. Davis picked up her finished dress, she promised to tell all her friends about the new shop and its very talented young designer.

Just as things were going well for Abby, Allen Tabor dropped in one day while Margaret was out of the shop.

"I may have made a mistake when I let you go, so I want to make amends and let you come back to work for me." He put on his most charming smile because very few could resist it, especially the girls.

"I don't think I'm interested, Allen. I'm happy here. As much as I like your mother, I don't want to go back to work for you." Abby refused his offer.

She didn't trust anything Allen said, so she wasn't about to put herself in that position again.

"But you have to! The new girl isn't working out, so we need you back there. I'll even give you a raise if that is what it takes." How dare this girl refuse him!

"I'm sorry, but I just don't want to go back. I like what I am doing here." Abby wasn't moved by his plea.

"It's a good offer. It might be in your best interest if you consider it. I'll come back in a few days to get your answer after you've had time to think it over." Allen stared at her for a moment before he turned on his heel and stalked out, clearly upset with the turn of events.

Abby shivered when he left. She had a feeling he didn't like to be turned down, so she was more than a little concerned about his next visit. She hoped Margaret would be there when that occurred.

Allen showed up a few days later again at a time when Abby was there alone.

"Well, have you decided to accept my offer?" He confidently strode up to where she was seated.

"I haven't changed my mind, Allen. I'm satisfied here and have no desire to go back to work for you." Abby tried to make her position very clear.

"So you are satisfied here, are you?" Allen answered thoughtfully. "Do you have any idea how quickly a reputation can be ruined, especially for someone who's just getting started in this business? A few of the right words dropped in the right places can bring you down along with this little shop you are so happy with." Allen's words terrified Abby right down to her very core because she didn't doubt he would carry out his threat.

"I'll give you the weekend to think things over. You have until Tuesday to accept my offer." He turned and confidently sauntered out of the shop, leaving Abby in a state of shock.

She wanted to tell Margaret about the threat, but first she needed to talk to Sheryl. Maybe she would have an idea as to what she should do.

Sheryl picked her up at the usual time. On the way home, Abby poured out the whole story to Sheryl. She hadn't mentioned it earlier because she thought she could handle the situation by herself. Now she knew better.

"I think this is too much for us to handle alone. Perhaps we should get Doug involved in the situation. Allen sounds dangerous, and I don't think he would hesitate to ruin your reputation if you turned down his offer." Sheryl was frightened for her friend.

"Can't we do something without involving my brother? The first thing he will want me to do is quit my job and move back home!" There had to be something else!

"Would you rather have your reputation in shambles?" Sheryl could see no other way.

"I guess you are right." Abby sighed. "I'll call Doug tonight."

When she called home, her father answered. She visited with him for a while, then asked if Doug was there so she could say hello to him before she hung up.

She told her brother to call her back because she needed to talk to him but swore him to secrecy because she didn't want her dad to know anything about the situation.

A few minutes later, Doug returned her call, quite curious as to what she wanted to discuss.

Briefly, Abby brought her brother up to date about her visits from Allen and his threats.

"I met Tabor once. He didn't impress me at all. Yet I am still surprised he would try to pull that kind of stuff on you. After all, he did fire you, didn't he?" Doug was incensed that somebody would make such threats against his little sister. He most certainly would try to put a stop to such shenanigans. "I probably need to come down and have a talk with him."

"There is another reason behind my dismissal. I will fill you in when you get here." She had hoped not to have to relate that part of things to him, but it was time for honesty. Doug needed to know the whole story.

"Did he mention when he would be back?" Doug asked.

"He said he would be back to see me on Tuesday."

"I'll be there Sunday afternoon so we can come up with a plan. In the meantime, try not to worry because we'll take care of Mr. Tabor and his threats."

***

Doug had Witt with him when he arrived Sunday. They had dropped their things off at a nearby motel because they planned to be there for as long as it took.

The guys had worked out a plan of action by the time they arrived at the apartment. They laid out their idea to the girls. Since Sheryl had the next day off, they enlisted her to take them to where they could get the equipment they were going to need. Abby was to tell Margaret about Allen's threats and get her permission to install a camera in the shop.

By Monday evening, everything was in place, and on Tuesday morning, they put their plan in action. Not about to be left out, Sheryl took Tuesday off work. Witt and Sheryl took up their hiding place in the storeroom in the back of the shop in case Allen should show up early.

They already had Abby wired for sound, and a second recorder was in the desk drawer, ready to be turned on.

His other visits had occurred just after Margaret left the shop for her lunch, so they didn't look for Allen until he saw Margaret leave the store. She had been instructed to circle to the back of the storeroom and reenter so she could hear what was said when Allen talked to Abby.

Doug paid an early morning visit to the Tabor shop. He hoped to have a conversation with Georgia before Allen showed up.

"Mrs. Tabor, do you remember me? I'm Abby's brother, Doug. We met when I came by a couple of times to see her," Doug greeted Georgia.

"Of course, I remember you, Mr. Andrews. How is Abby getting along? I was so sorry when she decided to quit her job here."

"She is doing very well at a new shop. How is her replacement working out?"

"She isn't nearly as talented as Abby was. But at least she is still here. That says something because, in the past, the designers I've hired never seemed to stay very long. Allen says they are all an unstable lot. But it is so difficult to build up clientele if you have to hire a new designer every two or three weeks." Georgia bemoaned her problem.

After their conversation, Doug was pretty sure Georgia knew nothing of Allen's antics.

"I'm so sorry about your troubles. Well, I won't keep you. I was just passing by and wanted to say hello. There's Allen. I'll just have a word with him before I go." Doug followed Allen to the backroom of the shop, out of Georgia's hearing.

"Tabor, I'd like a word with you." Doug closed the door behind him.

"Hello, Andrews. What can I do for you?" Allen knew exactly what Doug wanted.

"I want you to stay away from my sister. She's happy where she is and will never come back here, so you are wasting your time. I guarantee you will regret it if you try to ruin her reputation," Doug threatened.

"I don't know what you are talking about. I haven't seen your sister since she quit her job here." He had made sure there were no witnesses when he went to see Abby, so it was just her word against his.

"Just keep it in mind. If anything happens to my sister or her reputation, I'm coming after you." With that, Doug left the Tabor shop and returned to Margaret's shop as quickly as he could.

Margaret left at her usual time, and about five minutes later, Allen came in as if he didn't have a care in the world. He sauntered up to the desk where Abby was seated.

"Your brother paid me a visit a little while ago. Surely you didn't think a few empty threats from him would scare me off." Allen chuckled at the thought of it. "Have you thought over my offer? It's the only way you can save your reputation. Trust me, you will be happy working for me. Plus there will be fringe benefits as long as you behave." Allen had no doubt she would give in. It was only a matter of time, and she would be his.

"No, Allen. I haven't changed my mind. I won't ever work for you again. I like it here, so this is where I'm staying." Abby gave Allen her answer.

"I think it would be in your best interest to reconsider. All I have to do is drop a few words in the right places, and you won't be able to get a job making doll clothes." This girl was being more stubborn than he expected.

Abby leaned slightly forward and adjusted the desk drawer a little more open. It was a movement that did not go unnoticed. Allen reached across the desk to slide the drawer farther open in order to see what was inside. He retrieved the recorder Witt had placed there the day before.

"Surely you didn't think you two rubes from the sticks would be able to outsmart me, did you? Nice try, but it didn't work. What else do you have in your little bag of tricks? Bring it on. You will never outdo me. I'm too smart for you." He dropped the recorder to the floor and crushed it with his boot heel.

"Now we are back where we started. No witnesses and no proof. It's your word against mine. Are you ready to do as I say yet?" Allen knew he had won, and it was only a matter of time until she would admit it to herself.

"Oh, I think there are witnesses," Doug corrected Allen as he, Witt, Sheryl, and Margaret stepped out from their places in the backroom. "If you will look up in the corner by the ceiling, I believe you will see a surveillance camera. You did exactly what we hoped you would and destroyed evidence, all caught on camera. However, we do still have your own words provided by the wire Abby is wearing."

"What are you going to do?" Allen stood slack jawed. How could this have happened? He had been so careful not to get caught.

"For the time being, not anything," Doug answered his question. "I had a chat with your mother this morning before you came into her store. I don't think she has any idea what you have been up to with her former employees or why they really left. If I hear even the slightest hint of a rumor that your present employee leaves for any reason other than she wants to, I will give the district attorney everything we have gathered as proof of your shady activities as well as sworn affidavits from the five of us. I'm sure we will have no trouble finding other witnesses that you have wronged. Is that enough proof for you?" Doug asked.

"Now, I am going to suggest you go back to your mother's store and behave like a good little boy from now on, or we'll see whose reputation is in shambles," Witt joined in.

Abby walked to the door and held it open. Allen looked defiantly at the group. He knew he had been beaten, and all he could do was leave quietly before they changed their mind.

"Margaret, we thank you for allowing us to use your shop for this little sting operation." Doug hugged Margaret as they all let out a collective sigh of relief.

"Are you kidding? That's the most excitement I've had in years." Margaret was thrilled.

"By way of thanks, I would like to leave that camera in place. You never know when something else exciting might happen in here," Doug offered.

"Thank you. I appreciate having a camera, but I doubt that anything can top what happened here today. Personally, I'm hoping for a very quiet future." Margaret thanked Doug.

"This has been a busy day, so why don't you young people all go out and celebrate your victory before it's time for Doug and Witt to head home? I'll see you in the morning, Abby."

"Wouldn't you like to join us, Margaret?" Abby hated leaving her out of the celebration.

"No, thank you. I've had my excitement for the day. I'm going have my own little party with a cup of tea, a cookie or two, and my feet propped up."

The four friends went out for an early dinner before they parted company.

"Do you think we got the message across to Mr. Tabor?" Sheryl voiced what was uppermost in all their thoughts.

"Oh, I think he got the point," Doug answered. "I'm quite sure, basically, he's a coward, so I doubt he will take any chances of being exposed for what he really is."

"Thank you, Witt, for being here to help me out." Abby gave him a brief hug of appreciation.

"You know, now that it's over, it was kind of fun. I can't remember ever enjoying myself as much as I did today." Witt grinned at Abby, very happy to be sitting beside her. That was rapidly becoming a favorite spot for him, or at least one of his favorites. Actually, anywhere near Abby would do. Now that Tracy was out of the picture, maybe he still had a chance with her. He certainly was going to do his best to win her hand.

CHAPTER TWO

$\mathscr{B}$usiness flourished at the little shop as Abby's reputation as a talented designer grew. Most of their business was generated by word-of-mouth referrals given by satisfied customers.

True to her word, Margaret gave Abby a raise and offered her a percentage of the business. Abby decided that for now she would be happy with her raise and the 10 percent of the profits she was receiving. Margaret agreed but said the offer was still on the table if she ever changed her mind.

Doug called Abby one morning as the girls were getting ready to go to work. He told her that their dad had suffered a heart attack. The medical helicopter was getting ready to take off with him on its way to Denver. He was driving straight to the hospital, and Witt was already on his way to pick her up to take her there.

Sheryl stopped by Margaret's to tell her Abby would not be in that day. Margaret was sympathetic when she heard about Lay and asked Sheryl to tell Abby to take as much time off as she needed but requested they keep her up on Lay's condition.

By the time Abby and Witt arrived at the hospital, the staff was preparing Lay for surgery. Doug and Abby were permitted to see him for a short time before they were ready for him in the operating room.

"So you both are here. I'm glad. They tell me I need an operation. I didn't plan on that. Don't suppose you can get me out of it?"

He was nearly asleep, so they had to listen very closely to understand what he was saying.

"Of course, we're here. We wouldn't want to be any other place." Abby choked back tears as she gave her dad a kiss on the cheek and Doug patted him on the shoulder.

"We'll be here waiting for you when you get back. Take it easy." Doug squeezed Lay's hand.

After walking as far as they could with their dad, they returned to the waiting room, prepared to have a long wait. A very distinguished-looking gray-haired man came into the room where they had been directed to wait. He introduced himself as Dr. Daniel Woolery, Lay's doctor. He told them he would be assisting the surgeon. He said they wouldn't know just how long the operation was going to take until they got a close look at the damage to Lay's heart. In all probability, it would take several hours.

Witt kept Doug and Abby supplied with coffee and occasional snacks. Doug made some phone calls. Abby thumbed through magazines but had no idea what she was looking at.

A nurse came in often to give them updates. Each time, she told them the surgery was progressing well.

Sheryl came later in the afternoon with sandwiches for everyone. Just as they were finishing their food, Dr. Woolery came back to talk to them.

"He came through the operation in good shape. There was quite a bit of damage, but I think we were able to repair it all, so I don't see any problem with a full recovery. However, he will need a great deal of physical therapy. He can do that either at a rehab facility, or if he prefers, I think daily physical therapy at home would be acceptable, provided the therapist is skilled at the type of exercise Mr. Andrews will need."

"When can we see him?" Doug was the first to speak.

"They are getting him settled in ICU right now. That will take a little while. Someone will come get you when he is ready. Family only and just one at a time for now." The doctor turned to leave. "He will have some machines connected to him. They are routine and only temporary, so don't let them worry you. All things considered, he really is in good condition. I'm guessing he was in pretty good shape physically before this happened, and that works in his favor."

"He has worked hard for most of his life. This was the last thing we expected to happen to him." Witt spoke for Doug and Abby.

Abby was allowed in to see Lay about thirty minutes later. She was shocked at how pale and vulnerable her dad looked, lying so still with all the machines and tubes hooked up to him. It was all she could do not to cry. Instead, she smiled at him when he noticed her presence.

"Wow. They really have you hooked up to a lot of stuff, Dad. I bet you couldn't move your little finger without the nurses knowing about it," she gently teased him.

"Are all these necessary?" Lay looked up at what he could see of his attachments.

"The doctor told us they are only temporary. Actually, he said that the fact you are in such good health will help you get well faster." She leaned in close to hear his voice.

"I've worked hard all my life. Guess that's turned out to be a good thing."

"Before you know it, you'll be done with all this stuff and up and around again."

"Doug is waiting to see you, so I'll leave now and see you a little later." She kissed her father's forehead before she left.

Doug left to see his dad as soon as she returned to the waiting room.

"How is he doing?" Sheryl asked.

"He looks so small and so sick." was all she could get out before the tears came. Immediately, Witt's arms were around her, offering quiet comfort until she was able to regain control of her emotions.

"I'm sorry," she apologized as she withdrew from the comfort of his arms.

"No apology necessary. I'm here to help any way I can." He gave her his handkerchief to wipe away the last of her tears.

"How about I see if I can rustle up some ice cream for all of us?" Witt remembered that ice cream had always been Abby's favorite comfort food.

"I doubt you will find anything here as late as it is," Sheryl commented.

"Then I will go out somewhere. Never fear, I will come back with ice cream for all of us," Witt promised. "Sheryl, do you want to go with me? Between the two of us, we should be able to locate a good ice-cream store somewhere."

True to his word, before long, they returned with milk shakes all around just as Doug returned from his father's room.

Abby felt much better emotionally when it came time for her to see her father again. He looked better, and his voice was much stronger, so she didn't have to force her smile as she talked to him. All too soon, it was time for her to leave so Doug could visit.

Dr. Woolery stopped by to talk to them again. He said Lay was doing very well and suggested they go home for some rest. He assured them that should anything happen, they would be contacted immediately, but he didn't anticipate any problems at all. He told them Lay would remain in ICU for another day at least and then be moved to a private room on the cardiac floor until it was time for him to be released.

Reluctantly, they decided to follow the doctor's advice and leave the hospital. Doug and Witt took rooms at a hotel near the hospital. Sheryl had packed a change of clothes and a few other things she thought Abby might need, so she opted to take a room there also. Sheryl needed to go to work the next day, so she went home after they promised to call often and keep her updated.

After an early breakfast, they all hurried back to see how Lay was doing. Abby was pleasantly surprised to find him much improved and complaining to anyone who would listen.

Some of the machines were gone, and Lay had a little color in his face. As soon as he saw Abby, he started grumbling again, trying to get her on his side.

"They tell me I'm well enough to sit on the side of the bed but not well enough to have some decent food. How am I going to get any better if they won't give me something worth eating?"

"I'm sure you will get something when it's time. You've been through quite an ordeal. You have to be patient." Abby tried halfheartedly to console her dad. If she hadn't been so happy to see him looking so much better, she would have felt sorry for him. "I'm going to leave for a few minutes so Doug can come in. I know he will be surprised to see you looking so well."

"He seems a lot better this morning. Good enough to complain to anyone who will listen," she happily told them. "I told him you would be right in, so I expect you will hear all about it." She gave her brother a gentle push toward the door, feeling a great deal more lighthearted than when she left the hospital twelve hours ago.

"He's back." Doug returned after his visit with Lay. "It's actually good to hear him complaining. I'll never mind his grumbling again."

Doug and Abby embraced each other, very relieved at how much their father's condition had improved.

"Come on, you two. We were worried about him too. Don't we get a hug?" Witt wasn't about to miss this opportunity to put his arms around Abby again. He was quite sure Sheryl wouldn't object if Doug's arms found their way around her in the process.

The guys stayed at the hotel the next night, but Abby went home with Sheryl after Witt promised to pick her up early the next morning.

By the time they got to the hospital the next morning, Lay was feeling so much better that plans were underway to move him into a private room. Doug made arrangements for him to have a private nurse for the first two days.

After he was settled in his new room and the nurse in place, Doug and Witt left for a quick trip home for fresh clothes. Abby had them drop her off at the store so she could catch up on her work. They would all meet at the hospital that evening.

Margaret was happy to see Abby. She insisted on hearing all about the operation.

Lay was happily eating his dinner while sitting in a chair when they arrived back at the hospital.

"I finally got some decent food. It's not much, but it sure beats the heck out of that gelatin and broth stuff I got before." Lay was obviously feeling much better and already making plans. "I'm not going to be here very long. I'll soon be ready to go home and get back to work."

"Dr. Woolery says you will need to have some physical therapy before you can return to your normal routine," Doug reminded him.

"I won't need any therapy once I get back to the ranch and my regular work." Lay knew what he needed, and it was not somebody telling him how to do things. He had managed to take care of himself for fifty-some years, and he wasn't going to let some upstart try to run his life now!

"We'll have to have a long talk with Dr. Woolery about that before you go home." Abby had a premonition of trouble between her dad and any therapist who would try to insist on setting up an exercise regimen for him to follow.

It might be a good idea if she were home for a while, so she and Doug together could see that Lay did the therapy the doctor said he needed. She was going to have to learn a little about the process so she would be able to explain to him why he needed the specific type of therapy that was necessary to rebuild his heart muscles. If he did that, it would lessen the chances of his having a second heart attack.

How was she going to keep the job she loved and see that her father had the help he needed?

Maybe Sheryl would have a suggestion, or perhaps Margaret would have some thoughts. There had to be a way. She just needed to figure it out.

She decided not to mention her quandary to Margaret because she desperately hoped to formulate a workable plan of her own before discussing it with her boss.

"Why don't you ask Doug and Witt for their advice? They came through for you before, so maybe they can again." That was the only suggestion Sheryl could think of to help her friend.

"What could they do to help? I just can't be in two places at once. The only way we can see that Dad gets the help he needs is for me to be there to help Doug make sure that happens, and the only way I can keep my job is to be here at the store every day." Abby knew what she was going to have to do. There was no other answer. She would choose family over work anytime.

Maybe if she just asked Witt and Doug for their input... no, it would be a waste of time. They would feel sorry for her, but that was as far as it would go. Ultimately, it was going to have to be her decision to make.

Even so, when Witt picked her up after work that evening to take her to the hospital, she explained her dilemma to him.

"I'm sorry. That's a tough decision to have to make. Maybe we can put our heads together and come up with something, but right now, I don't know what the answer is." Witt had no idea what she should do. He was going to have to think about it. He couldn't let her down. There had to be a way for her to keep her job and help her dad at the same time.

That was what she more or less expected to happen, so she decided not to discuss it with Doug because the end result would no doubt be the same.

Lay was feeling and looking better every day. He was sitting up to eat all his meals.

"Dr. Woolery stopped by this morning. He says I'm doing so well that I can start thinking about going home in a few days." He couldn't wait to share his good news with Doug and Abby. "He asked me where I wanted to do my physical therapy. It didn't take me long to tell him, once I got back home, I wouldn't need any of this therapy he keeps talking about. I will get all the exercise I need working on the ranch. He still thinks I need somebody to watch over me. I've been looking out for myself for a lot of years and got along just fine. No need to make any changes now. He said, before I could be dismissed, he wanted discuss the situation with all of us."

"Dad, I understand that you will need physical therapy every day to build up your heart muscles. We have plenty of room. Why don't we see if the doctor can find someone who could live there and oversee your therapy for a little while?" Abby made a suggestion.

"Live there? Why on earth would I want someone there to watch my every move? I told you I can take care of myself! Doc said the surgery fixed what was wrong with my heart, so what else is it going to need?" Lay demanded.

"Dad, they did fix your heart, but now some of the muscles have been compromised. A therapist will know how to build up those muscles so they will be as good as new." Doug tried his hand at inducing Lay to accept physical therapy.

"Well, can't they just tell me what to do? I can take care of things myself if they show me how."

Lay was beginning to realize he might not get his way this time. When Abby and Doug joined forces, he knew he didn't stand much of a chance of getting his way. He never had in the past, so why would this be any different? Maybe it wouldn't be so bad to have someone help for a few days at least. As soon as he learned how to do things, then he could send the therapist packing. The whole thing shouldn't take more than a few days. Certainly, no longer than a week. He could put up with anything for that long if he had to!

Doug contacted Dr. Woolery's office to see when it would be convenient for a meeting and to ask him about a live-in therapist for his dad.

At the appointed time, they all met in Lay's room two days later.

"Like I told you, Doc, when I get home, I will take care of myself. I'll watch my diet and be careful not to overdo for a while. But it won't take long for me to get back to normal." Lay had no doubt of his recovery.

"Do you want to have another heart attack and go through all this again? Next time, it probably will be worse!" Dr. Woolery had a little straight talk for his patient. "Your heart muscles have been so weakened that they must be restrengthened in the correct manner, or they will fail you again. There are a number of muscles involved, and it takes someone like Edward Bennett to teach you how to bring each one of them back to capacity. It's going to take time to accomplish that. It can be done, but you must let him show you how."

Lay realized that he probably wouldn't be allowed to leave the hospital without some type of therapy in place, so he was going to have to agree to whatever Dr. Woolery wanted. He wasn't happy about it but was sure it wouldn't take long, and maybe it would get everyone off his back if he agreed to whatever they wanted him to do—for now.

"I have already spoken with Mr. Bennett. He's a fine nurse-therapist, and he is going to stop by this afternoon to meet you, Mr. Andrews. If you feel you can work with him, then I see no reason why you can't leave by the end of the week." The doctor rose to leave then added, "I'll leave you a list of instructions before you are released. They will include things you need to know about your diet and some limitations on your activities for a while."

"We'll keep an eye on him, Doctor," Abby spoke with more confidence than she felt. She knew her dad well enough to suspect he had something up his sleeve because he gave in far too quickly. She knew now that she was going to have to be home to help Doug make sure her dad did whatever the doctor recommended. It broke her heart, but she knew that she was going to have to quit her job because her father needed her.

"I've been thinking about you, your job, and your dad. I have a suggestion that might solve your problem." Witt offered as he took Abby back to work.

"I'd be grateful for any help." Abby welcomed his input.

"What would happen if we set up a video connection between your house and Margaret's store? That way you could be in direct communication with her every day. We could set up a fax machine for transmitting documents, and maybe you could go in to work only when you needed to be there in person. It shouldn't take too long to get your dad straightened out." Witt laid out his plan.

"I'd have to talk it over with Margaret, but I don't know why that wouldn't work. As a matter of fact, it's positively brilliant." Abby could have hugged Witt had he not been driving. Maybe she could still have both worlds.

"I knew there had to be a way. I just had to think about it for a while." Witt was already planning what equipment they were going to need and how to hook it up.

"The next thing we need to do is get you a good car so you can commute when you have to."

"I've been thinking about that. Do you suppose that you or Doug would have time to go car shopping with me?" Abby knew it was time for her to have her own transportation.

"Whenever you have time, I'm available. I imagine Doug will want to go with us. Between the two of us, I expect we will be able to find just the right car for you." Witt assured her they both would be glad to help her.

Margaret readily agreed to Abby's plan. They decided she need only come to the store on Thursdays and Fridays to start with. If something came up, she would be available on other days, but two days a week would be sufficient for now.

Her dad returned home by the end of the week. Edward arrived at the same time. Abby had been introduced to Edward earlier at the hospital. She found him to be a very personable young man who knew very well how to deal with stubborn patients. As soon as Edward got Lay settled in his room, he went to check on the exercise equipment he had asked to be delivered to the house the day before. As soon as he was satisfied that everything he needed was in place, he settled himself into what was to be his room for the duration of his stay. His room and Lay's had an adjoining door so he would be close should his patient need help.

***

She had been home for almost a week when she ran into Tyler at the post office one afternoon quite by accident.

"Abby! I didn't know you were back home. Are you here to stay, or is this just a visit?"

"I'm not sure how long I will be here. It depends on how my dad's recovery goes." Abby was glad to see him. She had refrained from asking anyone about him. She thought it better if she didn't know anything about his life now that he was engaged to be married.

"Do you have time for a cup of coffee? I would love to catch up on how your dad is doing and what's been going on in your life," he asked hopefully.

"I can stay a few minutes, and then I need to get back home." She knew she should say no, but what could it hurt? It was just a cup of coffee.

Tyler escorted her to the café next door, and while they waited for their drinks, he gave Abby his news. His engagement to Jennifer had been called off. He knew it was probably for the best, but he had been lonely since she went back to Denver.

Her heart leapt with joy at his words! Maybe she still had a chance with him after all!

Tyler asked about her dad's health and inquired about what she was doing in Centerview.

Before they parted, he asked her out to dinner that evening. She hesitated to give him an answer. She kept thinking about Witt, who had been a true friend to her during recent events.

But she had been in love with Tyler for so long…

She couldn't find it in her heart to turn him down, so she accepted his invitation.

She spent hours picking out just the right outfit for the evening. It had taken six years for this first date, so everything had to be perfect.

She was almost ready when Doug knocked on her bedroom door.

"He's here." Doug disapproved of her going out with Tyler but, so far, had held his tongue.

"Thank you. Tell him I will be right down." She hurriedly finished arranging her hair, picked up her wrap, and went down to meet Tyler.

They went to a restaurant on the edge of town, and while they were waiting to be served, Tyler opened the conversation.

"I liked you when we were in high school, but I was too bashful to ask you out. I saw you out with Witt Spenser a few times, so I assumed the two of you were dating," Tyler confessed.

"Witt asked me out occasionally, but we never did actually date." Abby tried to explain her relationship with Witt. She wasn't exactly sure what it was herself.

"I'm really glad you came back. I've been so bored since Jennifer left. Now you can keep me company." He reached across the table to lay his hand on hers.

"Jennifer wanted me to move to Denver and get a job, but Dad expects me to take over the ranch someday, so he needs me here for when that time comes." Tyler explained why he felt the need to stay at the ranch.

"Dad has spent the last few years preparing Doug to take over our ranch. He works every day with the ranch hands so he can understand what it takes to operate the business," Abby said. "Now that Dad has been incapacitated for a while, Doug is able to take over and run things."

"I've never actually had to do any work on the ranch." Tyler explained his philosophy on the day-to-day operation of the ranch. "I don't see any reason to actually do any physical labor. All I have to do is be able to hire competent workers, give orders, and keep the books. That shouldn't be too difficult." He sat back, full of confidence.

"I think there might be a little more to it than that." Considering how hard Doug worked, there must be more to it than merely issuing orders. But she made no further comments on the subject.

She went out with Tyler as often as she could, relishing every moment with him.

It generally was very late when he took her home, so most nights, she fell into bed completely exhausted.

Time was of no importance to Tyler because he could sleep until noon if he wished, but Abby didn't have that luxury. She had far too many responsibilities to attend to.

The working arrangement she had planned out with Margaret was running smoothly, but it took up much of her time. Thursday's and Friday's, she went to the store for her 'in person' appointments. She spent Thursday nights at Sheryl's, a plan Tyler complained about often. He wanted to drive to Centerview on Thursday nights to see her, but she vetoed that because she often worked late Thursday and had to be in the store early on Friday in order to complete all the tasks she had waiting for her to do. She knew from experience that he would keep her out far too late for her to be able to function as she needed to the next day.

She needed to spend time with her dad every day. As he began feeling better, it took all Doug and Abby could do to keep him from going back to work on the ranch. His daily therapy was going well, but it didn't take long to complete, so he had a lot of spare time on his hands that he didn't know what to do with. Being idle was something foreign to him.

Some days, nothing would please him. The only person who escaped his wrath was Mrs. Barry.

She was an excellent cook, and her meals were sometimes the highlight of his day. He went out of his way to be nice to her, and in return, she made special dishes for him. Quite often, she would prepare a between-meal snack, and sometimes he would ask her to join him on the front porch, an arrangement that seemed to please the both of them.

As often as she had time, Abby would take her dad around the ranch on an ATV so he could see firsthand that things were running smoothly.

Every evening, Doug would go over the plans for the next day's work with him.

As long as Lay felt he was included in the operation of the ranch, he was reasonably content to do as he was told.

Tyler kept demanding more and more of her time, saying he was bored when they weren't together. She occasionally shirked some of her work in order to spend extra time with him, but it was never enough.

Then one day she heard Jennifer was back in town!

A few days later, Abby went to the drugstore to pick up some medicine for her dad when, quite by accident, she ran into the one she considered to be her nemesis.

"You're Abby Andrews, aren't you?" Jennifer approached her.

"And you must be Jennifer Winslow. I heard you were back." Abby turned to face her.

"Tyler told me he was passing the time away with one of the local girls until he could talk me into coming back. I thought it might be you." Jennifer sized up the one person whom she considered to be her archrival.

THE DESIGNS OF LOVE

"I'm surprised you came back at all. According to Tyler, you hated it here so much that you couldn't wait to get back to the big city." Abby couldn't resist repeating what Tyler had told her.

"And I thought you had left the ranch for good to go to the big city to make your fortune. But I guess the minute you heard I was gone, you came running back to see if you could snag my boyfriend," Jennifer fired back. "I just needed a little time to think things over and let Tyler realize how much he missed me. It may take a while, but I will still get him to move to Denver and get a job. In the meantime, I will take care of Tyler's needs, so he won't be calling you again. It might be best if you went back to that little dress shop you work at in Centerview. Good day." With that and a shrug, Jennifer turned on her heel and walked out of the drugstore, leaving Abby stunned at what she had just heard.

Abby couldn't wait to get back to the privacy of her bedroom so she could think. Jennifer had obviously done her homework. She was going to be a formidable adversary. A part of her wanted to call Tyler to tell him what Jennifer had planned for him, but the rest of her thought he deserved what he got if he was dumb enough to take her back.

Doug noticed her downcast face and poor appetite at dinner that evening but decided not to comment on it. He had heard that Jennifer was back, so he guessed that had something to do with the state his sister was in.

After a week without hearing from Tyler, she guessed Jennifer had won. She was considering her next move when Doug knocked on her bedroom door.

"Would you care to talk about what's been bothering you?" he asked as he made himself comfortable in a chair near the one Abby was curled up in.

"I assume you know Jennifer is back." Maybe it would help if she could get her brother's take on the situation.

"I heard something about it."

"I ran into her at the drugstore last week. She as much as told me to get out of town. She said she had plans for Tyler and didn't want me to interfere with what she had in mind."

"What sort of plans?" He couldn't resist asking.

"She's going to marry him and then insist on him moving to Denver and getting a job. She has no plans to live here in Everett, ever."

"Good luck with that. He's never worked a day in his life, not even on the ranch, so I can't see him working anywhere else," Doug commented dryly.

"I don't know what to do. Dad's getting better every day, so I think you can handle him now. Maybe it's time for me to go back to Centerview." Abby sighed heavily.

"Is your work going okay the way you are doing it now?" Doug asked.

"Actually, it is working out very well. Business is picking up, so at some point, I may need to spend a little more time there, but for now, it's all right."

"I've never known you to be a quitter, so why are you thinking about it now? Are you going to let some newcomer drive you away from your home?" Doug asked.

"It's not that I'm running away. It's just that it might be better if I went back to Centerview," Abby reasoned.

"Better for whom?" Doug asked thoughtfully. "For you or Tracy or Jennifer?"

"I don't know," Abby answered quietly.

"If you truly want to leave, then perhaps you should. But make darned sure you are leaving for the right reason—not because you are running away from something or somebody, but because you are sure it's best for you," Doug cautioned her.

"In case you are interested, I'm planning to keep on seeing Sheryl, so I will still come visit you once in a while if you decide to leave. I might even bring Witt occasionally." With that parting shot, Doug grinned at her as he prepared to make his escape.

"I love you, Brother. Now go away so I can think about things." She returned his grin as she threw a pillow at him just as he ducked out the door.

After a lot of thought, she decided she needed to stay put for the time being. If she left, it would be akin to conceding victory to

Jennifer, and she wasn't about to do that. She wouldn't give up on Tyler just yet. Maybe he would wise up to Jennifer's plan and eventually come back to her.

She was willing to wait awhile. Meantime, she would not hide from them. When she met them, she would face them with her head held high and let the chips fall where they may.

CHAPTER THREE

Witt, having heard about Jennifer's return, visited Doug one day to ask him how things were going with Abby and possibly visit with her for a little while. He got his chance when she joined the men on the porch with a pitcher of iced tea and a plate of cookies.

"I'm thinking about calling Sheryl after a while to see if she is going to be free Saturday. Abby, would you like to go along for the ride if I go?" Doug asked.

"I'll be there Thursday and Friday anyway. I could stay over Friday night, if you're sure you won't mind a third wheel," Abby suggested.

"I have a solution for the third wheel. Witt, why don't you come along with me, and we can make it a foursome?" Doug couldn't resist a little matchmaking.

"That's an idea. What do you think, Abby?" Witt was all for it.

"It's fine with me." Abby didn't mind one little bit if Witt joined them.

"I'll call Sheryl, and if it's all right, we can leave about nine Saturday morning. If she's free, we could spend the night there and make a weekend of it. How would that be?" Doug asked.

"I'm game. Is that okay with you, Abby?" Witt was happy at the prospect of spending two days with Abby.

"That's a great idea!" Abby was surprised at the surge of happiness she felt at the thought of spending a weekend away from the ranch. Or was it because Witt was going to be there?

Sheryl made reservations for the guys at the nearby motel and got tickets for the group to attend a dinner theater for Saturday evening.

She took them sightseeing in Denver Saturday, visiting places they hadn't been in years. The guys' favorite was the Museum of Natural History, but the girls liked the Art Museum best. By the time they finished the tour, it was time to go to the theater.

Sunday morning, they had brunch at a local restaurant, followed by an entertaining game of miniature golf, where the girls trounced the guys handily.

All too soon, it was time to return to the ranch, but not before they promised to spend another weekend together very soon. Besides, the guys insisted on a rematch at miniature golf.

***

When they arrived home, Abby learned Tyler had called a couple of times, leaving messages that he needed to talk to her. He wanted her to call as soon as she got home.

Upon hearing of Tracy's attempt to reach his sister, Doug sought her out, intent on having a serious talk about her conduct in recent weeks.

He found her in her bedroom, staring out of one of her windows across the rolling hills, watching a couple of young antelopes playing their version of tag.

"Do you have a minute to talk?" he asked as he entered the room and took a seat.

"Of course, I was just thinking about Tyler. I guess I should give him a call to see what he wants." She turned from her place in front of the window to sit in a chair across from Doug. "What's on your mind?" Abby asked, more than a little curious about Doug's visit. He rarely set foot in her room, so it must be important.

"I've never said anything to you about whom you dated in the past, but I think it's time to discuss this situation with you—Tracy and Witt." He hesitated, not quite sure how to proceed. "You once told me you fell for Tracy the first time you saw him. What were you? Fourteen?"

"Yes. I was a freshman in high school. Tyler transferred there when his parents bought their ranch. The first time I laid eyes on him, I knew he was the only one for me. I had hopes of getting his attention right up until the time he announced his engagement to Jennifer." Abby smiled wistfully as she recalled that first time she saw Tyler.

"Well, Witt would kill me if he knew I was telling any of this to you, so I wish you would keep it just between us," Doug cautioned her. "Witt once told me he has been in love with you since the first time he saw you in sixth grade. He has always known how you felt about Tracy, but he hoped you would get over him." Doug paused briefly.

"It never once occurred to me that Witt was anything more than a friend and neighbor. I am so sorry. I would never intentionally do anything to hurt him." Abby felt terrible.

"He knew you were using him when you accepted dates with him, but he didn't care. It allowed him to spend time with you. He made a point of only asking you to places he knew Tracy would be to ensure you would go," Doug added. "When he heard Tracy announce his engagement to Jennifer, he hoped it was finally going to be his time. He didn't count on you leaving town before he could do anything about it."

"Oh, Doug. I feel so bad about everything. How can he not hate me for the way I've treated him?" She thought she couldn't feel any worse, but now she did.

"Well, you're back in town. Tracy is apparently still engaged, so what are you going to do about Witt?" Doug got to the reason for his visit.

"I honestly don't know what I'm going to do. I've been in love with Tyler for so long. I had no idea how Witt felt." Abby needed to do a lot of thinking before she talked with either of them.

For the first time in a long while, Abby poured her heart out to Polly that night. Not that she expected an answer, but it sometimes helped her think if she could put her thoughts into words. She was at a loss as to what to do about Witt. Certainly, she was very fond of him, but she had only thought of him as a friend or brother, not someone to be romantically involved with. In hindsight, she had certainly taken advantage of him over the years, an action she truly regretted.

After a sleepless night of tossing and turning, she was no closer to coming to a decision. Maybe if she returned Tyler's call, it might help her make up her mind. Perhaps he wanted to say good-bye because he was going to marry Jennifer. Maybe he would tell her he had broken up with Jennifer and wanted her back. The only way she was going to find out was to call him, but no matter the answer, someone was bound be hurt.

When she finally summoned the courage to make the call, she was surprised at the result.

Tyler's parents were having a patio party the next Saturday evening, celebrating the happy couple's reunion and their upcoming nuptials. All the neighbors were invited. Every fiber of her body wanted to say no, but she was going to have to face them sooner or later. Maybe it would be easier if there were some friends around.

"I'll talk to my dad and brother and let your mother know." She gave him a noncommittal answer so she would have time to think about what she wanted to do.

"Please try to come. I need to talk to you." Tyler wanted to see her again.

She knew she had to attend the party. If she stayed away, it would raise eyebrows because it was a small community and when someone had a party, everyone attended.

It would be so much easier if she could go with a date. Her first thought was to ask Witt, but that was out of the question. She had used him far too many times already.

She went in search of Doug to tell him about the party, but he already knew.

"Witt called a little bit ago to see if Dad was planning on going. I asked him, and he said no. He didn't feel up to dealing with a crowd yet. So Witt's coming by to pick me up. You are welcome to join us if you want."

"I know I should go, but I'm really not looking forward to spending the evening watching Tyler and Jennifer fawn all over each other." She was in a quandary.

"How would it be if I put in a good word for you with Witt?" Doug suggested, half in jest and half because he thought he understood her dilemma.

"Don't you dare! I've taken him for granted far too many times already." That would have solved her immediate problem, but she was ashamed to ask Witt for anything more.

"How about if you hang out with me while we are there? I won't mind," Doug offered.

"Tempting as that might be, hanging out with my brother won't solve my problem. I'm going to have to face this by myself. Maybe it won't be as bad as I think." She just wanted to get the evening over with.

In the end, she accepted Witt's offer of a ride. It was better than arriving alone.

The first person she ran into upon her arrival at the party was Jennifer.

"I'm surprised you have the nerve to show up at my party," Jennifer spoke quietly so no one could overhear what she was saying to Abby. "I told you to stay away from Tyler. He's mine, and I have plans for him. I don't need someone like you spoiling things for me. If you are smart, you'll just turn around, get back in your car, and go home where you belong. Or better yet, go back to Centerview, and stay there!"

"There you are! I'm sorry it took so long to park the car. Is this Tyler's fiancée? Hi. I don't believe I have had the pleasure." Witt slipped one arm around Abby's shoulder and extended the other to shake hands with a dumbfounded Jennifer. "I'm Witt Spenser, Abby's escort for the evening." Witt bent down to give Abby a kiss on her cheek.

"Witt, this is Jennifer Winslow, Tyler's... ah... friend." Abby finally got her voice back. She couldn't bring herself to call Jennifer Tyler's fiancée, so *friend* was as close as she could get and still be polite.

"It's nice to meet you, Jennifer. Congratulations on your engagement." Witt gave her a broad grin, then turned to Abby.

"Let's go circulate, honey. I see some people I haven't talked to for a while. Excuse us." With a nod to Jennifer, he steered Abby across the lawn to where Doug stood visiting with some friends.

"Mission accomplished." Witt gave Doug the thumbs-up sign.

"Don't tell me you put Witt up to that!" Abby couldn't be angry at Doug for trying to help her.

"Well, it wouldn't have looked right for your big brother to come to your rescue, so Witt was all there was left." Doug grinned and winked at her.

"Well, Jennifer was not being very welcoming, I'll say that, and I do appreciate your help defusing her. Actually, that expression on her face when she saw Witt was priceless." Abby was beginning to see a little humor in the situation.

Jennifer remained glued to Tyler's side for most of the evening, doing her best to be sure he didn't get a chance to have a private word with Abby.

It was nearly time to leave before Tyler got a moment free to talk with Abby. He pulled her aside to a secluded spot so they could have some privacy.

"I'm really glad you came tonight." He moved close to her as if he wanted to put his arm around her, but he didn't touch her.

"I've really missed our conversations. We have so much in common that it's easy to talk with you. Do you think we could still meet once in a while just so we can talk?" he asked hopefully.

"You do realize that Jennifer would never allow that, don't you?" Abby was surprised at Tyler's request.

"Oh, I know, but she doesn't have to know anything about it. She's leaving in the morning for Denver to work on the wedding plans. She'll be gone for two or three weeks, so I will have plenty of time for you. We can go someplace where we won't be seen. All I want to do is talk. What's the harm in that?" Tyler coaxed her.

"Tyler, as long as Jennifer is in the picture, I won't be a party to such behavior. I can't deny I enjoyed our time together, but I will not carry on with anyone who is about to be married to someone else!" Abby was insulted that Tyler thought so little of her morals.

"I get so lonesome when Jennifer is gone. What's wrong with two old school friends having dinner and conversation occasionally? That's all I'm asking for." Tyler tried to reason with her.

Why couldn't she get him out of her heart? He had been uppermost in her thoughts for so long that he had become much like a bad habit she was struggling to control before it ruined her life or, at the very least, her reputation.

In the end, the bad habit won out. She finally agreed to meet him for dinner a few days later. She drove her car to the back of a parking lot on the edge of town. He was waiting when she got there. They went to a small secluded restaurant a few miles out of town, where she had a very enjoyable evening.

Tyler was his most charming self. He kept the conversation entertaining and lighthearted.

As soon as the meal was over, he took her directly back to her car without delay. He made no mention of wanting to see her again.

By the time she arrived home, she was wondering what she had done wrong to cause him to decide not to see her again. Would he call her, or should she call him to tell him how much she enjoyed the evening?

She rationalized there was nothing wrong with what she had done, so why not do it again if he asked? After all, it was just a dinner.

After a sleepless night, she knew what they had done the night before was wrong, so she resolved not to see or try to contact him again.

Tyler called her several times every day, but she didn't pick up his calls. A week later, while she was at the bookstore, picking up some copy paper, he followed her into the store.

"I've been trying to talk to you. Why haven't you picked up my calls?" he demanded.

"I really don't think it's a good idea for us to sneak around. It's best just to make a clean break of it." It was difficult for her to tell Tyler that, but it was the right thing to do.

"Can't we go to that café across the street and talk it over with a cup of coffee?" He took her hand in an attempt to pull her along.

"A cup of coffee won't change my mind. Besides I just don't have the time. Margaret is waiting for me to fax some papers to her."

Tyler left the store while she was paying for her purchases. He was standing beside her car when she returned to it.

"Please, will you go to dinner with me one more time? I think I may be about to make the biggest mistake of my life, and I really need your advice. Can't you give me a couple of hours of your time? My life is on the line," he pleaded.

"What kind of a problem could you possibly have?" It seemed to her that he was in a pretty good place in his life.

"It's too complicated to talk about here on the street. Go to dinner with me, and I will tell you all about it." He knew he had her intrigued. "It is going to affect the rest of my life, so I need you to help me make the right decision." That ought to reel her in.

"Why don't you talk it over with Jennifer? She should be able to help you better than I can." She knew she was weakening. She also knew it would be better for her if she turned him down, but her heart wouldn't let her.

"Jennifer is part of the problem, so I don't want to mention it to her until I have come to some kind of decision. Please, I'm desperate. Help me out this one last time."

"I guess it won't hurt to have dinner with you one more time, but it will have to be the last time. Is that clear?" Abby relented.

"Thank you. You may be saving my life." He grinned. "What time can I meet you at the parking lot tonight?"

"I can't make it tonight. How about at six tomorrow evening? She knew it was wrong the minute she uttered the words, but she couldn't help herself.

"Good. I'll be waiting for you." Tyler strolled off, very pleased with himself.

She told Doug she was going to dinner and a movie with a girl-friend so he wouldn't ask questions she didn't want to answer.

Tyler was waiting in the parking lot at the appointed time.

"I'm so glad to have this time with you. No one understands me the way you do. I've made reservations at the Ramada Inn for us." Tyler explained where they were going after they passed the restaurant they had eaten at previously.

"Tyler! I am not going to a motel with you! It's at least fifty miles out there, and that's just too far to go for dinner!" She strenuously objected to his plans. "I think you had better just turn around and go back to that little restaurant we just passed where we had dinner at before!"

"It's okay. I don't mind driving because they have an excellent chef, and the food is well worth the drive. Jennifer and I ate there once. No one will know us there, so we will have complete privacy." He reached over to pat her on the knee.

"Just how much privacy are we going to need?" A chill ran down her spine. She hoped she didn't have cause to regret this evening.

"I just want to talk about my life and what I should do with it. I really need your input."

"Are you sure that's all it will be? Just dinner and conversation?" Why didn't she trust him?

"Absolutely! Only a meal! After that, we can decide together where the conversation will take us." He crossed his heart in an effort to convince her.

"I can tell you exactly where the conversation is going to take us. We are going to eat dinner, and then we are going straight home!" She had to put a stop to any plans he might have made for her. "Now suppose you tell me about this mistake you are about to make."

"The only reason I'm marrying Jennifer is because I'm being pressured into it. My mother and her mother were sorority sisters in college. They recently got their heads together and decided Jennifer and I would make a good match. So we are getting married because of our mothers and not because we are in love. They agreed it was time for us to make them grandmothers." Tyler explained his problem.

"They can't force you to get married! This is still a free country!" Abby had never heard of such a thing.

"You don't know her mother! She is so overbearing that she has Jennifer completely under her thumb, and she has convinced my mother that it's the right thing to do. They're so wrapped up in their plans that no one, including Jennifer, will listen to me. The only thing I can think of to do is run away, but then how would I get by without money?" For once, Tyler sounded defeated.

"That's the most awful thing I've ever heard of." Abby couldn't believe what she was hearing. She didn't have a clue as to how to advise Tyler except to tell him to break the engagement.

**

The restaurant was very busy by the time they got there, but they were immediately taken to a very secluded alcove.

A bottle of champagne was waiting at their table, and Tyler had already ordered their meal. Just as the staff was bringing their salads, Tyler remembered he had left his wallet in the car. He told Abby to go ahead and start because he would only be gone for a moment. It wasn't going to take him very long to do what he needed to do.

Abby had barely begun eating her salad by the time he finished his task and returned.

Despite her misgivings, Abby enjoyed her meal. The food was superb. Tyler was charming and funny. Soon she began to relax and have a good time.

"It's getting late. I expect we had better be heading home pretty soon." Abby looked at her watch, surprised at how late it actually was.

"Can't we stay just a little while longer? I don't know when I've enjoyed an evening as much as I have this one. I can be myself when I'm with you." He wanted to delay their return to the car as long as he could.

"We still haven't talked about how you can get out of your engagement." She was having such a good time she almost forgot why they were there. "I guess we can talk about it on the way home."

"I'd rather be someplace where I won't be distracted by driving." Tyler stalled for time. "Why don't I see if I can get us a room some- where here for an hour or two? It would be quiet there, so we could think and talk without interruption."

"Absolutely not!" There was no way she was going to allow him to get her into a motel room.

"The rest of my life is at stake! Can't you give me a few more minutes?" he pleaded with her.

"If you were truly concerned about your future, it seems to me that you would have been more anxious to talk about it. We had all evening to discuss it, and apparently you chose not to, so it's too late to begin a conversation here. We will have plenty of time in the car on the way home." She remained adamant.

It was time to go to plan B.

"If you insist on leaving, I guess I can wait another day, but you have to promise to have dinner with me tomorrow evening so we can discuss things." Tyler signaled for the check.

"I don't know if I can get away tomorrow evening, but we can have dinner one night soon," Abby promised, relieved that Tyler had agreed to go.

Tyler assisted Abby to her seat in the car, took his place behind the steering wheel, and turned the key to start the car. When it failed to start, he got out and raised the hood as if looking to see what the trouble was. After stalling for an appropriate amount of time, he returned to his seat.

"I can't imagine what is wrong. It's never failed me before. It's too late to call my mechanic tonight. I don't suppose you have anyone to call." He tried to sound dejected.

"No. I don't want anyone to know where I am." She tried frantically to think what to do. "Isn't there someone you can call to come pick us up?" She knew she should call Doug. He would have come to get her, but she didn't want him to know how stupidly she had behaved.

"I can't think of anyone. I didn't actually want anyone to know what I was doing either."

"I'm sorry, but it looks like we're stuck here. I guess the only thing to do is get a room for the night, and then see about getting the car fixed in the morning. Wait here, and I will explain the situation to the motel office and see if I can get us a room." He opened the door to get out of the car.

"Get two singles. I'll pay for my own room." She hoped they were on opposite ends of the motel. She had just about all she could stand of Tyler this evening. She had a nagging suspicion that the car situation didn't just happen, but for now, she was going to give him the benefit of the doubt.

"I'm sorry, but they only had one room left, and it's a single. I figured it was better than spending the night in the car. We can make do, can't we? It's just for tonight." He grinned at her. This was working out very well so far.

"Could you call the office to see if they can send us a cot?" Abby asked as she surveyed the very small motel room equipped with only one double bed, two chairs, and a dresser.

"I asked when I got the room. All their spare cots are in use. I guess we will have to share the bed. We can manage for only one night, can't we?"

"No, that won't be necessary. I'll make a pallet on the floor." It was bad enough they were forced to share a room. Thank heavens no one knew where she was.

She found a robe and slippers for each of them in the closet so at least she wouldn't have to sleep in her clothes. The robe would do nicely.

While Tyler was taking his shower, she called housekeeping to ask for a couple of extra blankets and sheets. When folded, the blankets would soften the hard floor.

By the time Tyler finished his shower, she had made herself a pallet in the far corner of the room. She draped the extra sheet across the backs of the chairs to give her a little bit of privacy.

She went to take her shower, leaving Tyler surveying her sleeping quarters. This was not at all what he had planned!

When she emerged from the bathroom, after making sure the sash of the robe was securely knotted, she found him sitting glumly on the side of the bed.

"Well, you finally have the privacy you thought you needed. Do you want to talk about your life now?" Once again, she broached the elusive subject.

"Come sit with me." He patted a space on the bed next to him as he smiled at her hopefully.

"I'm fine over here." She sat perched on the edge of one of the sheet-covered chairs.

"It will be easier to talk if you're not clear across the room from me. Come. Join me," he reiterated. Patting the space next to where he was seated on the bed once again.

"I can hear you just fine from here." They couldn't have been more than nine feet apart. "Now suppose you tell me what you want to do about Jennifer."

"It's like I told you. I'm not in love with Jennifer. I never have been. She just wants to get her mother off her back. If our getting married is what it takes, then she's all for it." He paused a moment, then continued, "We talked about it once. If it would make our mothers happy, then we could go through with the ceremony. It will be strictly a marriage of convenience. She wants to give her mother a couple of grandkids, and then we will quietly get a divorce and go our separate ways. That way, everybody is happy, and then I will be free to marry for love."

With an innocent look, he turned to Abby for her approval of his plan. "I'm hoping you will understand my position in all of this and meet me once in a while just to let me cry on your shoulder."

"Let me get this straight. You want me to see you on the side while you marry someone else for convenience. And when you decide to get a divorce, then what happens? Would I be in line for wife, or would I remain status quo while you look for a more suitable wife number two?" Abby could only shake her head at what she was hearing. "I've heard of arranged marriages. But in my wildest dreams, I didn't think they would ever be as cold and calculating as what I have just heard!" Abby decided they deserved each other. How could she have been so wrong about him?

"You make it sound so much worse than it really is. It's not like I want to do things that way. If I don't go along with their plans, my folks might cut off my money. Then how would I live? If you would only let me see you once in a while—just to talk. That's all I want, honest, just a sympathetic ear. No one understands me like you do," Tyler pleaded his case.

"I don't believe you know me at all. Certainly not if you think for one second that I would be party to such a plot! As far as I'm concerned, you are making your own bed, and you will need to lie in it with your own wife! Now, if you will excuse me, I'm going to retire for the night."

She lay down so abruptly that she banged her head on the floor. Why hadn't she asked for an extra pillow when the maid brought the blankets?

"Abby! Please at least think about it. I can't get through this mess without a friend to talk to." Tyler had been so sure he could talk her into going along with his plan. After all, apparently she had been in love with him for years. He picked up on her feelings shortly after he transferred to her school. He threw her a few crumbs occasionally just to string her along. He didn't need her then, now he did. She couldn't turn him down. He knew she would come around; it just might take a little longer than he expected, but she would come around. He was sure of it!

After a night of tossing and turning on her makeshift bed, Abby was extremely relieved when morning finally arrived. She was up and dressed long before Tyler stirred.

She waited impatiently for him to get dressed. He needed to make arrangements for someone to fix the car so they could get home.

"If you will get us a table for breakfast, I will take a quick look at the car. Maybe I can see something I missed in the dark last night." He sent her on ahead to the dining room.

In short order, he came back with good news. "I found out what was wrong! I had the car serviced yesterday. Apparently, the fellow who worked on it failed to put a couple of wires back on tight enough, so they came loose. I saw them as soon as I raised the hood. I'm going to have a talk with his boss when we get home. I don't want this happening to anyone else."

"It's a shame you didn't see them when you looked last night." She was pretty sure he knew about them last night, but still she kept her own counsel for the time being.

"Well, let's have breakfast and get on the way home. I don't know just how I am going to explain my absence." Abby had to think of something.

"You're an adult. You don't have to explain your actions to anyone," Tyler countered.

"No, I don't have to, but it's common courtesy to let your family know if you are going to be gone overnight," Abby corrected him.

They made the trip home in relative silence.

She spent the time trying to come up with a logical explanation for her absence. She was glad she hadn't mentioned which one of her friends she was going to be with.

Tyler was working on a new strategy to get Abby to fall in with his plans. So far she was being obstinate. He came up with several plans, all of which he rejected for one reason or another. This was turning out to be more difficult than he expected, but there was no doubt in his mind that, in the end, he would get her in his bed. He just had to be patient.

***

"We missed you at breakfast," her dad greeted her as she arrived home.

"I'm sorry, Dad. I didn't plan on staying overnight, but the movie was so late getting out that I decided to stay with my girlfriend instead of driving home. I should have called, but it was so late I knew you all would be in bed."

"It's all right." He accepted her apology. "I expect there is probably some breakfast left if you are hungry."

"Thanks, but I grabbed a bite earlier." She was anxious to escape to the solitude of her room.

"If you happen to go to town sometime today, would you mind getting some things from the drugstore for me while you're there?" he asked.

"I'll be glad to. I need an ink cartridge for my printer anyway. I'll pick up your list before I go."

Two hours later, she arrived in town. She decided to get the things her dad needed first and drop them off at the car before she went on to the bookstore.

When she returned to her car with her dad's items, Tyler was waiting there beside it.

"I saw your car and figured you wouldn't be far away," he greeted her with a broad grin as if nothing had happened. "I need to talk to you. How about I pick you up for dinner this evening?"

"No, Tyler. It's over. You killed anything I thought I felt for you last night." Abby was a little surprised that she felt no regret at that declaration.

"I thought we had a good time last night. What's the matter?" He didn't expect that.

"I'm not as naive as you seem to think. It took me a while to figure it out, but I have no doubt that you are the reason your car wouldn't start last night and then miraculously started this morning," she blurted out the accusation.

"I just wanted to take you somewhere so we could talk and not be interrupted. Was that so wrong? Anyway, nothing happened." He tried to reason with her.

"I should never have been there at all," she responded.

"But you are so comfortable to be around that I feel I can tell you anything and you will understand what I'm feeling. You are so good for me. Please don't be mad," he pleaded with her.

"Tyler, you are getting married soon. The only person you need to be talking to is your fiancée. If you can't do that, then you have a problem that I can't help you with." She reached around him to open the car door.

"You can't be serious! I won't let you go! I need you!" This wasn't in his plans at all.

"Please don't try to contact me again. I regret that I wasted so much of my time thinking about you in the past, but now it's over. Good-bye, Tyler. I hope you have a good life." She dropped her package in the front seat, closed and locked the door, turned on her heel, and walked away without a backward glance, leaving Tyler speechless and in shock.

***

She felt strangely lighthearted as she finished her errands and returned home.

This might be the time to return to Sheryl's apartment and her job. She was considering when to make the move that evening when a sharp knock at her door interrupted her thoughts. A very solemn Doug entered her room.

She had a bad feeling when she saw the somber look on her brother's face.

"I just intercepted a phone call from a very angry Katherine Tracy." Doug wasted no time getting to the point as to why he was there.

"What did she want?" There was no doubt in Abby's mind about the direction the conversation was going to take, but still she had to ask.

"Would you care to explain to me what you were doing at the Ramada Inn Motel fifty miles from here with Tyler Tracy last night and again this morning?" He made himself comfortable in his chair, prepared to stay until he was satisfied with her explanation.

"I'm sorry. I had no idea we were going to a motel. I thought we were going to a restaurant just outside of town. He said all he wanted was someone to talk to. He thought he was about to make a big mistake, and he wanted to talk about his options. It was supposed to be dinner and conversation. That's all. I swear!" She tried to explain her conduct.

"Whatever possessed you to spend the night there?" Doug was struggling to remain calm as he asked his questions.

"We did go to the car to come home, but it wouldn't start. He said it was too late to call his mechanic, so he got a room for us. Nothing happened. I promise!" She desperately needed for him to believe what she was saying.

"Oh, I believe you. I give you credit for having more sense than that. The question is, will other people believe your story?" He was pretty sure that, given human nature, they wouldn't.

"Do you think everyone will find out?" She was pretty sure she already knew the answer to that question also.

"Everett is a small town, and Mrs. Tracy is very angry. What do you think?"

"What am I going to do?" She was up pacing back and forth, trying to think. "I guess I could leave town until it blows over. Maybe I should go back to Centerview."

"*Now*, you want to leave town? If you had done that when you talked about it earlier, then your reputation wouldn't be going down the tubes today." Doug knew he had to help his little sister, but he didn't have any idea of how to go about it.

"It might be better if you didn't leave town right now. That would be tantamount to admitting your guilt. You are guilty, but Tracy deserves to share the blame with you. After all, the motel fiasco was his idea. We need to get that little fact out there. The question is, how do we go about doing it?" Doug was thinking out loud.

"Jennifer will probably come back to help spread the story," she added.

"It would be my guess she is already on the way. She's coming back to protect her property. The mothers probably already have a campaign in place to put the blame squarely at your feet and make Tracy an innocent victim who succumbed to your feminine wiles. They will probably say you have been in love with him since high school and you were making one last ditch effort to win him back while Jennifer was away, planning their wedding." Doug was pretty sure that was what was in store for Abby.

"But that's not true! I didn't do that! He asked me out to dinner—just to talk. I wasn't trying to get him back. I just felt sorry for him, I swear! In fact, I ran into him this morning while I was in town. I accused him of doing something to the car so it wouldn't start, and he didn't deny it. I told him anything I might have felt for him was gone and I didn't want to see or hear from him ever again. In fact, I told him if he needed to talk to anyone, then it should be Jennifer, not me. That's the God's truth!"

Doug had to believe her! He just had to!

"Oh, I don't doubt that is the truth, but how are we going to get other people to believe you? I think we are going to have to come up with a plan of our own, and the sooner, the better."

There had to be a way to derail the smear campaign he was sure they were mounting. The question was, how could they stop them dead in their tracks before they totally ruined Abby's reputation? There was no question about her being in the wrong with what she did, but people needed to hear her side of the situation because the blame should not be entirely hers.

"I think we need help figuring out what to do. I'll call Witt. Maybe he will come up with some ideas worth trying."

"Please don't bring him into this mess! It's embarrassing enough without him finding out how stupidly I have behaved," she pleaded.

"Do you really think he won't find out about it?" Doug asked. "If he hasn't already, I'm sure it won't be long before he hears the whole sordid tale. The question is, do you want him to hear your truth or the opposition's truth?"

"Speaking of finding out about it. Did Mrs. Tracy happen to mention how she heard about it so quickly?" Not that it mattered, but she was curious if Tyler had anything to do with it.

"She mentioned receiving a phone call a little while ago from Cara Baldwin. It seems she and Jack decided to celebrate their twenty-fifth wedding anniversary at the Ramada Inn. They saw you and Tracy in the dining room last night and again this morning. Evidently, she just couldn't wait until they got home to call Mrs. Tracy."

Abby slept very little that night. Her thoughts kept flitting from what had happened to what she should have done to what she was going to do to get herself out of her predicament.

Witt arrived very early the next morning.

"I am so sorry to involve you in my mess. I don't know how I could have been so stupid." She was near tears as she tried to apologize to Witt.

"We all make mistakes, Abby. Right now we have to get you out of yours." He couldn't help himself; he put his arm around her shoulders in an effort to comfort the distraught girl. His action brought her completely to tears, so he enveloped her with both arms and held her tightly until she regained her composure. It felt so good to have her there despite the reason. Doug thought he understood how his friend felt, so he remained silent until Abby withdrew from Witt's embrace in search of a handkerchief, which Witt immediately supplied.

"I guess the first thing we need to do is tell Dad what happened," Doug suggested.

"Better he hears it from me than someone else." She handed the slightly damp handkerchief back to Witt, took a deep breath, and prepared to face her father. "Will you both go with me?"

Lay sat quietly throughout Abby's apology to him for having lied about where she spent the previous night and her confession of what really happened.

"I am so sorry, Dad. I didn't mean for any of this to happen. He told me he thought he was about to make a big mistake and needed someone to help him decide what to do. I honestly thought I could help. I had no idea we were leaving town, let alone going to that motel so far away. Then when we got ready to come home, the car wouldn't start. He said nobody would ever find out if we spent the night there. So he got a room for us. He told me they only had one room, so we would have to share. I spent the night on a pallet on the floor. He said he would call his mechanic the next morning about getting the car fixed. Like a fool, I believed him. When he went out to look at it the next morning, he said he 'found' two wires that had accidentally come loose, plugged them in where they belonged, and then brought me home." Abby dropped her head in her hands, totally at loss as to what to do next.

"We all make mistakes, honey. That's how we learn. The question now is, what are we going to do about yours?" For the moment, Lay was at a loss as to how to help his distraught daughter.

"I guess I probably should just pack up and move back with Sheryl until this all blows over."

"Is that what you really want to do?" Lay asked thoughtfully.

"No, but I've brought enough shame to this family. If I don't leave, it will just fuel the gossip." What else could she do but flee back to Centerview?

"And you think the rumors will just go away if you leave?" Doug asked.

"You haven't asked me, but I think leaving town is probably the very worst thing you could do right now. It might be better if you stayed and got your side of the story out. People need to be reminded that there are always two sides to everything." Lay wanted her to stay and fight. "Let's not rush into anything. We need to come up with a workable plan as soon as possible. We'll meet here again right after lunch. Maybe one of us will have a brainstorm between now and then. Don't worry, honey. Between the four of us, we'll come up with something." Lay slid his arm around Abby's dejected shoulders in an attempt to console her.

"I just feel so bad about everything. I've always considered myself a reasonably intelligent person, so how could I have done something so stupid? I'll never trust anyone again." Abby made a solemn promise to herself to never get caught like that a second time.

"Like I told you before, we're all human. We make mistakes. The trick is to learn from them but not go overboard. Granted, yours is a pretty big one, but in due time, it will pass. Trust me, they always do." Lay released her as the little group broke up, each combing their brain, trying to come up with a solution that would salvage Abby's reputation.

Abby went to her computer, intending to get some work done for Margaret, but all she could think about was that night and what else she could or should have done.

She had no appetite for lunch, so she settled for a cup of coffee on the front porch. She hoped the fresh air would clear her mind so she could come up with something—anything to help her get out of this mess she had caused herself.

She was still there when Witt returned.

"Do you want a cup of coffee while we wait for the others? There's a fresh pot and mugs on the table behind me," she offered.

"Coffee would be good. Where is everybody?" Witt asked as he helped himself to the coffee and a couple of the cookies Mrs. Barry had put out earlier.

THE DESIGNS OF LOVE

"Dad's finishing his therapy session, and I just saw Doug come out of the north barn, so he should be here pretty soon."

"How is your dad's therapy going? Is he still complaining about everything he has to do?" Witt asked after taking a drink of his coffee.

"Actually, it's going very well. He really likes Edward, so that makes him more inclined to do as he is instructed. I think he has come to understand the importance of the right kind of exercise, so that also helps."

By the time Doug arrived, Lay had finished his session with Edward and joined the others on the porch. Abby poured coffee for her dad and Doug while refilling her own cup.

They all sat quietly for a bit, enjoying the fresh air and quiet of the country.

"Well, did any of you come up with a bright idea?" Doug finally broke the silence.

His question was met with yet more silence until Lay finally spoke up.

"Well, I do have sort of an idea we might toss around. What would happen if we each made a list of the people we can count as our true friends, tell them the whole story, and ask them to get your version out there for everyone else to hear?" Lay waited for their reaction to his suggestion.

"That's better than anything I thought of." Witt was the first to answer.

"Sounds like a plan to me," Doug spoke up.

"We'd have to decide exactly how much I will need to tell them," Abby ventured.

"We have to tell them the absolute truth from your perspective. We can't blame Tracy for everything, but we need to make darned sure that people understand that he must shoulder part the blame and not look like the complete innocent I'm sure they will be claiming him to be." Lay knew they had to be truthful from the very beginning. It was too easy to get tangled up in a web of half-truths. Abby should not have put herself in that position in the first place, but she did, so perhaps she should take the larger part of the blame.

Still in Lay's mind, Tracy was equally as guilty because his lies to Abby had in part caused the situation in which they were involved.

"I can talk to our friends, but do you think they'll help get the word out to anyone else?" Abby was still a little skeptical.

"Let's get the lists made first and then call them. Tell them Abby needs their help with something. Time is of the essence, so get as many as you can to come over this evening. Try to get the rest of them here tomorrow evening. It will be easier and faster if you can explain your side to everyone at once rather than one at a time." Lay's reasoning made sense.

"Also, if they are here, we might be able to gauge their reaction. Hopefully, they will all help, but at any rate, we might get an idea of where we stand by the end of the evening." Doug added thoughtfully. At this point, they had nothing to lose.

"What if they don't believe anything I say?" Abby asked.

"You just tell them what happened in a straightforward manner without embellishment. If they are the real friends we think they are, then they can't help but believe you." Witt tried to encourage her.

"Everyone has always known you to be a truthful person. Why would they think you have reason to change now?" Doug agreed with Witt.

"Let's get started on our lists so we can get this over with." As Abby passed pencils and pads to each of them, she asked, "How many people do you think we should try to reach?"

"I don't think that matters as much as making sure we can trust the ones we choose. I'm going to look specifically at people I've known most of my life, like the ones I went through school with." Doug weighed in on the question.

"If you have known them all through school, then you should know which ones you can depend on no matter what. That's who you are looking for." Lay could count on his fingers the people he would trust with his life. They were the ones he was going to call.

Each of them sifted through their group of friends and narrowed their lists to include only their most trusted ones.

Within the hour, they all were on their phones, offering invitations. Most of the people could be there that evening. The rest would attend the next night.

Abby retired to her room to think about what she was going to say. This whole thing was going to be embarrassing for her, but she had only herself to blame for it all. She decided to lay out the whole story as it happened and let the chips fall where they may.

She had so many butterflies that she barely touched her dinner. Would seven o'clock never get here? She paced the floor because she was too nervous to sit anywhere for more than a few seconds.

"Come sit with me while we wait." Lay thought he understood what his daughter was going through. He wished he could help her, but it was something she had to face herself. "You do know that you are not going through this alone, don't you? Doug, Witt, and I are squarely on your side. In a little while, I think you will find you have more people on your side than not."

"Yes, I know. I don't think I could go through this without your support," Abby admitted.

"You know, I haven't lived this long without learning a little bit about life." He briefly hugged his daughter, then continued, "I've learned that every life has to have its ups and downs. You enjoy your ups, even celebrate them sometimes. You endure your downs because you know they will pass. The thing is to learn from the downs and come out a stronger, wiser person on the other side of them." He paused and then finished what he had to say. "I imagine you think this is the worst thing anyone has ever done. I guarantee you it's not. If you are very lucky, you will have a lot of ups and downs in the years to come. As time passes, this will only be a very small blip in the grand scheme of things. I promise you."

The doorbell rang, signaling the first of their guests had arrived.

"Now go upstairs, wash your face, and comb your hair. I'll call you when it's time for you to come down. When you do, you need to look calm, cool, and collected. Show them you're an Andrews and you can handle anything." Lay tried to give her encouragement.

"Thanks, Dad. What would I do without you?" Abby gave him a quick hug.

"You would get along just fine. You just need to always remember you are an Andrews. Be as proud of that as I am of you." He watched her leave the room with a little more spirit in her step than when she entered a few minutes earlier. He knew she would be just fine because she had her mother's spunk. One couldn't ask for any more than that.

***

Abby was able to get her nerves under control by the time Lay called her to come down. She managed to greet her guests in a calm and cool manner.

Mrs. Barry had already laid out refreshments for everyone to share while they waited to see what the meeting was about. Most of them had heard some of the rumors floating around. They wondered if this was why they were there, but they all held their own counsel until someone was ready to tell them why they had been summoned in such an urgent manner.

"I guess by now, you all have a pretty good idea why we're asking for your help this evening." Lay got the meeting started. "Abby made a mistake, a pretty big one. I'm hoping you will listen to what she has to say and form your own opinion as to where the blame should lay. Abby, the floor is yours. Explain what happened."

Lay took his seat as Abby stood to confess her actions two nights earlier.

She related the happenings in a calm, concise manner. Everyone listened attentively while she laid out the whole sordid story. She included the trouble with the car but made no comment as to why it failed to start. She told them about their meeting the day before and that she would not be seeing him again.

"So now you have my side of this situation. I hope you can help me get the truth out. I haven't heard what's being said about me, and I know I must shoulder the larger part of the blame, but I should not have to carry the entire burden because there are two of us in the wrong. Thank you for listening. Does anyone have any questions?" Abby was prepared to make further explanations if necessary.

Witt, Lay, and Doug had spent the time Abby was talking trying to discern the expressions of their guests. Unfortunately, they were mostly inscrutable. So it was hard to tell what the people were thinking. They could only wait for their reactions.

"Well, knowing Tyler Tracy as I do, I'd say that little weasel would lie his head off to get what he wanted." It was the first comment to be made.

"Did he go out to the car by himself for anything while you were in the restaurant?" someone asked.

"Yes, he said he left his wallet in the car. He was only gone a couple of minutes though," Abby answered.

"How long would it take to yank a couple of wires out?" someone else wondered.

"You can bet they didn't fall out by themselves," someone said, causing a ripple of laughter.

"That little rat has been pulling stunts to get what he wants ever since I've known him," another commented.

"I don't know about the rest of you guys, but I can't wait to get Abby's side out there." This came from someone in the back of the room.

"I have to go to my women's club meeting tomorrow afternoon. I'll make sure they all hear Abby's side of this fiasco." This was from Witt's mother, Elizabeth.

"I've got a poker game tomorrow night," the local druggist chimed in. "I think we will have our own little gossip session."

Abby had no idea that there were so many who bore some kind of ill will against Tyler.

Most everyone offered an opinion on Tyler Tracy before they left. The vast majority were of a negative nature.

"If we work at it, I bet we can defuse the Tracy bombshell before it gets off the ground." This was another comment from someone as she was leaving.

Abby knew she wasn't out of the woods yet, but she was feeling a whole lot better than she did a couple of hours earlier.

"I'm proud of you, girl." Lay wrapped Abby in his arms, giving her a big squeeze as the last of her guests were leaving. "You did it! You won them over!"

"They did seem to believe me. Maybe they will help." Abby was praying they would.

"Of course, they will help. Didn't you hear them? They really don't like Tracy." Witt couldn't help but see a little humor in the remarks made about the man causing Abby so much pain. He shared their dislike for Tracy but probably not for the same reasons.

As Abby straightened the living room and carried the glasses and plates back to the kitchen, she realized she was starving. She had been too nervous to eat very much all day, so now she raided the refrigerator. She found some potato salad, sliced ham, and baked beans. Then she finished with a big slice of blackberry pie. She took a couple of cookies to her room to snack on later.

She slept well that night and was up early the next morning to get caught up on the work she should have done the day before.

A knock at her door interrupted her train of thought.

"Come in."

"Sorry to bother you." Doug stuck his head in the door. "Since you didn't come down to breakfast, I just wanted to check on you."

"Oh, I guess I lost track of time and didn't realize it was this late. I'll be right down." No wonder she was hungry; it was nearly ten and long past her normal breakfast time.

While she was enjoying her second cup of coffee, Mrs. Barry handed her a phone message Katherine Tracy had left for her.

"If possible, could you meet me for lunch today at Duggin's? About one o'clock. We have to talk, and it's important."

Her heart dropped to her toes as she read and reread those lines. What could she possibly want except to warn her from trying to see Tyler or suggest she leave town! It couldn't be a good meeting. Should she go alone or take a witness with her? Should she tell her dad or Doug? What if they insisted on going with her? She finally decided it would be better if she faced Mrs. Tracy by herself. She really didn't want any witnesses to what Mrs. Tracy most probably was going to say.

At the appointed hour, she nervously entered the restaurant to join her hostess.

"Thank you for coming. I wasn't sure you would." Mrs. Tracy opened the conversation.

"I almost didn't, but I guess we do need to talk," Abby responded.

"Would you like a drink before we order our food?"

"I'm not much on alcoholic beverages, Mrs. Tracy. Iced tea will do just fine," Abby requested.

"Please bring us two iced teas," Mrs. Tracy instructed the waiter, then turned back to face her table companion. "I prefer you call me Katherine, if you would. May I call you Abby?"

"Of course." Abby was expecting theirs to be a short conversation, so she had no objection.

They each studied their menus in complete silence. When the waiter returned with their drinks, he took their orders.

"Did you know that we almost lost Tyler when he was six years old?" Katherine broke the silence as they waited for their food.

"No. What happened?" Abby wished Katherine would get to the real reason they were there, but she wanted them to remain civil as long as possible.

"He got very sick, but the doctors couldn't find out what was wrong. We took him to one doctor after another. Not one of them had a clue as to what was wrong or how to cure him. Finally, he was so ill that the doctors had to come to him. His pediatrician told us they had done everything that could be done. He was sorry, but there was nothing left. It was out of their hands."

"One day, this new young doctor came into the hospital room and asked if we would permit him to take another look at our son. He said he had been studying some of the test results, and he thought he might have found something in one of the tests. He asked our permission to run two more tests. Of course, we gave it to him. At that point, we would have made a deal with the devil if it would have saved our boy." Katherine was quiet for a moment, then continued, "Two days later, he came back with some news. He had found something in the lab work that he didn't think should be there. It apparently showed up in only one test done previously, and that happened to be the one he looked at. He had seen this only once before, when he was in medical school. He told us he had contacted his former professor to see if the school still had the information about it. The next day, he came in with more news. The medical school professor was flying in with all the information they had, including possibly a treatment for the illness. That evening, they started a new series of IVs, each specially mixed by a chemist under the watchful eye of the professor. Within 24 hours, Tyler opened his eyes and looked at us for the first time in a week. By the end of the week, he was sitting up and eating soft food. Three weeks later, we got to take our healthy little boy back home."

Katherine smiled at the thought of that day. "I get down on my knees every day and thank God for sending that young doctor into my son's room."

"From then on, Tyler got anything he wanted. We were so thankful to have him back that we couldn't do enough for him. Too late, we realized we weren't doing him any favors. When we tried to say no to him on occasion, he would throw such a tantrum that it was just easier to let him have what he wanted. I'm sorry to say he doesn't always behave in the manner he should. I know he sometimes lies to get what he wants and he can be a handful if someone crosses him. His father and I know we are to blame for his behavior now, but at this point, we are at a loss as to what to do about it."

Katherine reached across the table to squeeze Abby's hand. "I was in The Book Store this morning and happened to overhear a couple of ladies talking about you and Tyler. Their version of what happened at the motel was a lot different than what I heard from him. I went straight home and asked Tyler what really happened. He admitted the motel was his idea and you knew nothing about his plans because, had you known, you would never have gone with him." Katherine explained why she was there.

"Thank you, Katherine, for your honesty. It does help." Abby breathed a sigh of relief.

"When Jennifer gets here this evening, I am going to tell her the whole truth. What she wants to do about Tyler is completely up to her. I would like for her to stay with him because I believe she would be good for him, but I will certainly understand if she decides to move on."

"As far as I'm concerned, the whole regrettable incident is closed, and I asked you here today to apologize for my son's actions and beg your forgiveness for the part Gerald and I had in causing it." Katherine waited for a response from Abby.

"Of course, I forgive you. I appreciate your telling me about Tyler. I think I understand a little more as to why this could have happened." Abby felt like a huge weight had been removed from her shoulders.

"Gerald and I have been talking to doctors about getting Tyler some help. They are thinking maybe some kind of therapy perhaps," Katherine explained.

"I know it seems like Tyler has it all, but underneath, I have always felt he was very unhappy. I'm glad to hear that you are trying to get him some help," Abby encouraged her.

"Our food is coming. I don't know about you, but I'm starving." Abby was anxious to close the subject and move on to happier topics.

"Jennifer tells me you have moved to Centerview and have a job in a dress shop." Katherine took the hint and was happy to move on also. "What do you do there?"

"I design special-order clothing. Mostly I do women's dresses," Abby answered.

"You actually design the outfits and then make them from scratch? That must be such interesting work." Katherine envied her. "I can't even sew a straight seam."

"Actually, I've made my own outfits for several years. To me, it's exciting when someone comes into the shop and allows me to fit her with a dress in a style that suits her shape, age, and personality. After we decide on the design, we pick out the fabric and color to be used. In no time, the client has a one-of-a-kind dress made especially for the occasion for which it is needed."

***

After what turned out to be a very enjoyable lunch, Abby returned home with a much happier heart. She was contemplating her return to Centerview when she entered the house. She was shocked to find a very subdued Tyler waiting for her. Where was his car? She hadn't noticed it. Her father was also there, looking like a thundercloud.

"Mother told me she had invited you to have lunch with her today." Tyler stood to greet her. "I understand she was going to try to straighten things out with you. That's why I'm here. I want to apologize for treating you so shabbily. I have no excuse except it scared me to think about getting married, and I guess I just wanted to have one more fling before I was going to be tied down for the rest of my life." Tyler sounded truly sorry.

"I did have a very enlightening conversation with your mother." Abby was beginning to see Tyler in a whole new light. "If you truly have doubts about marrying Jennifer, then you should have a talk with her. It really doesn't matter what anybody else thinks. You have to do what is right for you." Abby tried to encourage him.

"Jennifer's coming in this evening. Maybe we do need to talk things over. I need to think about what I want to do. I guess it's time for me to do a little growing up," Tyler answered quietly.

"There's no big rush to make decisions, Tyler. Think things through before you come to any major changes in your life." Abby extended her hand to Tyler as he prepared to leave.

"Thank you for listening to me. Again, I am sorry for everything. I can promise you it will never happen again." Tyler clasped her hand as he walked to the door.

"It's over now, so don't think any more about it. Just get your life in order before you do anything drastic. Thank you for coming to see me. Good-bye, Tyler."

"Thank you, Mr. Andrews, for not throwing me out even though I probably deserved it." Tyler turned to bid Lay good-bye before taking his leave.

"Good-bye, Tracy." Lay had no clue as to what had happened, but Abby did look happier.

Lay hadn't said a word while Tyler and Abby were talking. He just listened in amazement at what he was hearing. As soon as the door was closed and she turned to face him, he found his voice. "That must have been quite a conversation you and Katherine Tracy had while the two of you were at the restaurant."

"Yes. It was very illuminating. Katherine got Tyler's side of what happened. Then she overheard my side of it while she was at the bookstore this morning. She went home and got the truth out of Tyler. She apologized for everything. It's over, Dad. I think you can cancel tonight's meeting."

She gave her dad a peck on the cheek and fairly flew up the stairs to get some of the work done that she had been shirking.

She decided it was time to start thinking about going back to Centerview. Her dad seemed to be satisfied with his progress and more willing to do as he was told.

She happened to overhear her dad call Mrs. Barry Agnes one afternoon. They seemed to spend a lot of time sitting on the porch these days. She briefly wondered just how 'friendly' they were getting. She was going to see if Doug had noticed anything. Personally, she liked Mrs. Barry, but she hadn't ever thought of her as more than the housekeeper. Perhaps she should. It might be a good thing for her dad. It may even be beneficial for the both of them.

CHAPTER FOUR

*B*usiness at the store was increasing, and she really needed to be there. Margaret had been very patient; however, the client list was growing, requiring more and more of her time. All in all, she would be very happy to get back into the routine of going to work every day.

She called Sheryl to tell her she would be moving back to the apartment by the weekend. Doug and Witt offered to help her move back to Sheryl's the next Friday. They decided, since they were going to be there anyway, perhaps they should just stay for the weekend. Sheryl was all for it. She got their motel reservations and began thinking about things they could do while the guys were there.

Miniature golf was a must because, after their firm trouncing by the girls the last time, the guys were demanding a rematch. A tour of the capitol building or the US Mint might be fun. She hadn't been to Estes Park for a while. If the weather stayed pleasant, perhaps they could have a picnic somewhere. She didn't really care where they went or what they did as long as she could spend time with Doug. It was a shame they lived so far apart. She was really beginning to like him.

Lay told Abby that he would miss her, but he understood why she needed to go. He hugged her tightly and told her to be careful and call often and come back home when she could.

The move back to Sheryl's went smoothly, and by the time she got home from her job, the guys were settled in their motel and Abby was unpacked and everyone was ready for the weekend entertainment Sheryl had planned. Truth be told, Witt and Doug would have been happy anywhere as long as they were with Abby and Sheryl. They really didn't need to be kept busy. Sharing time with the girls was all the entertainment they needed to make them happy.

The one thing they were really looking forward to though was the rematch of the miniature golf game.

Saturday afternoon, they got their wish. However, they came to regret that wish because they lost again—not as badly as before, but still it was a loss. A little chagrined, they accepted their defeat gracefully, each quietly planning to find a way to practice on their golfing before demanding a rematch. And there would be a rematch. Of that, they were sure!

The weather was perfect by Sunday morning, so the group packed a lunch for a picnic in Estes Park. They found the perfect spot at one of the lookouts near the summit. After eating their fill, someone suggested a walk, but no one had the energy to get up, let alone walk, so they all were content just to sit and idle the time away with small talk. All too soon, it was time to return to reality and head home. It was nearly dark before the foursome said their reluctant good-byes.

***

It felt good to get back into the work routine. Abby hadn't realized just how much she had missed the thrill of starting with a blank piece of paper and seeing a beautiful dress come to life.

One morning, Margaret came in with news. She had received a phone call from her daughter, Carolyn. She had quit her job and was coming back home for a little while. Margaret didn't know the whole story, but she said that the girl apparently had her heart broken by someone she worked with and needed to get away for a while.

"It'll be good to have her home, if only for a little while. Surely, between the two of us, we can get her cheered back up. I'll try to get her to come here so she won't just sit at home and mope. I can't wait for the two of you to meet. I just know you will hit it off."

Two days later, Margaret's daughter accompanied her to work. Abby already knew a little about Carolyn. She was twenty-four, a graduate of a college in New York, and had a degree in fashion design. Upon her graduation, she had been offered a job at a very prestigious fashion house in the city. Abby knew the girl must be very talented to have been offered a position like that. Maybe she could learn something from Carolyn while she was there.

A small part of her couldn't help but wonder what would happen if Carolyn decided to stay and work with her mother. Margaret would be thrilled, but there wouldn't be enough work for a second designer.

She decided she would cross that bridge when she came to it. Carolyn would probably return to the big city as soon as she was feeling better.

"Carolyn, I would like you to meet Abby, the most talented designer in the state of Colorado. She's the reason we are doing so well." Margaret introduced the two girls.

"It's good to meet you, Carolyn. Your mother has told me a lot about you." Abby offered her hand in welcome.

"Thanks. It's nice to be back home. I'll try not get in your way if you will allow me watch you work. Maybe I can learn something." Carolyn gladly accepted Abby's hand.

"Wait, I was hoping I might pick up a thing or two from you since you have worked in New York City." Abby laughed.

The two girls immediately liked each other as Margaret was confident they would.

At first, Abby was a little embarrassed to have Carolyn watch her work, but she soon realized Carolyn was not there to criticize but to try to learn.

"Could you show me how to create the pattern from your drawing? I've never done that. It wasn't covered in my school. All they did was to show us how to draw. That's all I had to do where I worked. The patterns were made in a whole different department."

One day when her mother was away from the shop, Carolyn asked Abby, "Did Mother tell you why I decided to come home?"

"She told me you were coming home because of a man. She said that she thought he had broken your heart." Abby answered.

"Jeffery was our office gofer. He kept us supplied with things we needed to work with and delivered the finished products to the next department. I was thrilled when he asked me out to dinner one evening. He was so full of charm that I fell head over heels. It never once occurred to me to ask if he was married. Turns out he was, with two kids and another on the way. I found all this out by accident one day when I overheard one of my coworkers mention seeing a picture of Jeffery and his family and going on and on about how cute his wife and kids were. It seems everyone in the office knew except me, and no one saw fit to fill me in on that one little fact. I guess they all thought it was just one big joke. I couldn't stay there after that."

"People can be so cruel sometimes, but trust me, you will get over it." Abby's heart went out to her new friend. "Someday I'll tell you my tale of woe that first brought me here to Centerview, and then we can commiserate together."

"They say misery loves company. You tell me your story, and then we can decide who the bigger idiot is." For the first time, Carolyn was beginning to see a little humor in her situation. Perhaps she wasn't the only fool in the world after all.

***

Sheryl came home with news of her own one evening. Her supervisor, Mrs. Jones, had been offered the position of vice president in charge of Purchasing. If she accepted, she would be transferring to the corporate headquarters in Chicago.

"She recommended me as her replacement. Can you see me as a boss?" Sheryl asked.

"I can totally see you in charge. I think you would make a great boss. I'm happy for you." Abby was truly glad to see Sheryl get a promotion. She had certainly earned the job.

"I'm not sure it's mine yet. The corporate offices have to approve whoever is recommended. Mrs. Jones said she should hear within the week." Sheryl sighed. It was going to be a long week.

In the end, Sheryl was offered the job. However, there was a catch along with the offer.

"They want me to go to New York City for training. It will be a summer class offered at a midcity college and will last for eight weeks. If I want the job, I have to go. Can you believe that! I've worked there for four years. I think I know how things are done!" Sheryl really wanted the promotion but was reluctant to go back to school to get it.

"It's only eight weeks. It'll pass in no time. How much is it going to cost you?" Abby asked.

"It won't cost me anything. The company is paying for everything. There are dorms on the campus. They are mostly empty in the summer, so anyone attending summer classes is permitted to stay there." Sheryl relayed what she had been told.

"Then you have to go. Anytime you are offered free training, you should take it. You might be surprised at what you learn." Abby was going to miss her roommate, but she knew Sheryl had to go to New York City.

"I'll have to think about it. I'll see if I can find out more tomorrow." Maybe it wouldn't be so bad. She might even enjoy it. She just hated having to go by herself.

Carolyn had been home for almost a month. She seemed to be settling into a comfortable routine. She asked Abby if she could try her hand at designing a dress for one of their clients. It turned out beautifully, and the client was truly impressed when she tried on the completed dress.

That little voice in the back of Abby's head couldn't help but wonder if this was the beginning of a new job for Carolyn, and what was going to happen to her position? For now, all she could do was to wait and see how things went.

"I hear your roommate is in line for a promotion where she works," Margaret commented one morning as they were opening the store. "Helen told me about it last night. She said she had accepted her promotion and is going to move to Chicago in about four months. Has Sheryl made up her mind about going to New York City for that training session?"

"I think she is leaning toward going, but I'm not sure it's definite yet," Abby answered.

"Do you know where she will be taking her training?" Carolyn asked.

"I don't know exactly where it is. She said it was a midcity college. There are dorms on the campus for her to live in. I guess they offer a number of summer classes which anyone can take." Sheryl hadn't said much about the location.

"I bet I know where it is. I took a summer course there the first year I was in college. They offer a wide range of subjects. I took a course in fabrics, dyes, and color combinations. I was amazed at what I learned. I will try to get some brochures from there. Maybe I need to take a look at what else they are offering now. I might find something that will help me later." Carolyn decided that might be good if she learned something to help her get another job.

"I wouldn't mind looking at the literature from there too." Abby decided it wouldn't hurt to think about doing something to help her find another job if Carolyn decided to stay on in Centerview and work with her mother.

A few days later, Carolyn came in with a number of brochures from the college. She sent some of them home with Abby to see if indeed it was the same school Sheryl would be attending.

Sheryl had definitely decided to attend the training session, so that same day, she came home with some more information about where she would be going. It turned out to be the same as the school Carolyn had gone to.

Later that evening, as the girls were poring over the information, Abby came across what she thought was the course Carolyn had spoken about. That was a subject she had little knowledge about. It might help her if she took it. But she couldn't leave Margaret for that long if Carolyn decided to leave. But if Carolyn was staying, she probably wouldn't have a job for very long anyway. If only she knew.

"Did Sheryl have time to look at the stuff you took home last night?" Carolyn was curious if it really was the same school.

"Yes, it's the same. We both looked at the classes offered. We found the one she would be taking, and I think I found the one you took. It really sounds interesting. I wouldn't mind taking it some-day." Abby wished she could.

"We need to talk. Let's go to lunch together," Carolyn suggested.

Well, maybe she would have her answer after she talked with Carolyn. Abby was pretty sure Carolyn would be staying. What else could she want to talk about?

After a morning that seemed interminable, it was time for the girls to go on their lunch break.

After they ordered their food, Carolyn opened the conversation.

"Abby, I've been watching you work, and it amazes me. Basically, I've been working around designers for the last four years. I've learned that there are very few designers with natural talent. Most people who call themselves designers have been taught how to do what they do. They all must have a modicum amount of talent, but it has to be directed toward the art of design. As they are taught, each one of them picks up a certain style. If you are around designers long enough, it's relatively easy to look at a dress and identify the designer. There's always some little thing that they do every time they create a design. I've been watching you for the last month, and I can't find your 'tell'. Everything you do is different."

"Maybe, it's because I tailor the dress to the person. All people are different, and they need a style to fit them." Abby was pleased to hear what Carolyn thought of her work.

"That's what I want to do. At the job I had, I just cranked out designs. I never saw the finished product. I want to have that per-sonal touch. I want to feel all of the time the way I felt when you let me design that dress for Mrs. McDaniels. It was so great to see how happy she was with something I had a hand in creating."

"I know my mother would be very happy if I stayed here in Centerview and worked with her in her store. I really hate to disap-point her..."

They were interrupted by the arrival of their food.

"Where was I?" Carolyn was ready to continue their conversation.

"You didn't want to disappoint your mother." Abby was sure she knew where this was heading.

"Oh yeah. I really love my mother, and I was glad when she finally decided to open this store. I'm happy she found you to be there to help her make it a success." Carolyn continued, "I know I should stay here and help her like a good daughter, but I'd be stark raving mad in six months. I really am happiest when I'm in the middle of the hustle and bustle of New York City. I can't believe how much I miss it."

"You mean you don't want to stay here?" Abby's spirits soared at Carolyn's words.

"No, I don't. However, I have a proposition for you."

"What's that?" Abby waited for the catch.

"If you truly want to take that college course we talked about, I'll stay here to help Mother until you get through the training session. But as soon as you finish, you have to come back so I can get out of here."

"Carolyn, I could hug you." Abby was exuberant. "I was so afraid you were going to stay, and I knew there wasn't enough work for the both of us. So I figured I would be leaving." She couldn't wait to tell Sheryl they would be able to go to school together.

"Are you kidding? Mother can't get along without you. I'm so thankful you are here to take some of the guilt off of me. This way I can stay where I am in my element, and I know Mother is happy doing what she wants."

"Please don't mention our talk to Mother. I'll explain my plans to her later," Carolyn cautioned.

That night, the room-mates pored over the class schedules, trying to find the one that Carolyn took that would coincide with Sheryl's class. They finally found it, so Abby filled out an application to be mailed the next day. If she was accepted, they both would have two weeks to get ready to leave for school.

"I guess we will have to break the news to Doug and Witt that we won't see them for a couple of months if I get accepted." Abby hadn't thought of that.

"Doug already knows I'll be gone, and he is planning to fly back to see me sometimes. I would guess Witt will be right there beside him on that plane if you are there with me." Sheryl had already discussed the situation with Doug.

"Do you really think he would do that?" Abby had trouble believing Witt would be willing to fly anywhere to see her after the way she had taken advantage of him over the years.

"Of course, he will! He likes you, and you like him!" Sheryl teased her roommate.

***

The next two weeks were spent getting ready to leave for New York City. They spent one weekend at the ranch. Lay was pretty much back to normal. Edward had finished his part of the therapy and departed. He gave Lay an exercise plan for him to follow and promised he would come back occasionally to check on him.

The first night they were there, Lay asked to be excused because he had previously asked Mrs. Barry to go to dinner and a movie and he didn't want to disappoint her.

When Abby asked Doug how long that had been going on, he said they had gone out for the evening a couple of times.

"It's kind of funny. If they think no one is around, they use first names, but if anyone is within hearing distance, it's Mrs. Barry and Mr. Andrews."

"What do you think about that, Sheryl?" Abby had mixed emotions.

"It seems to me they are good for each other. It's got to be lonely for them once in a while, so if they make each other happy, why not?" Sheryl was a little surprised, but she could see no real problem with their going out for dinner and a movie.

"You are probably right. It's just going to take a little time to get used to it." Abby decided whatever happened, as long as they were happy, she guessed it was all right.

Mrs. Barry left ample food for their evening meal. After they ate an early dinner and cleaned the kitchen, Doug took them for a short tour around the ranch. He paused at the crest of the highest hill on the ranch so they could watch the sun go down.

"Sometimes I forget just how beautiful Colorado is. Then I watch the sun set like it's doing now, and I'm reminded why I love living here." Abby wished that perfect moment could last forever.

"This is my favorite spot on the whole ranch. I come up here every once in a while just to watch the sun go down. No matter what goes on in my life, I can always count on this hill to make me feel better." Doug had never told a living soul about that before. He didn't know why he did now except he wanted Sheryl to know. He couldn't figure out just why that was so important to him, but it was.

Sheryl didn't say a word; she just reached for his hand as if she understood how he felt.

"Well, I guess it's time to go." Doug broke the silence a few minutes after the sun sank out of sight. "It'll be dark soon."

It was an almost somber trip back to the house. Each of them was thinking about what they had just seen and the fact that it could be well over two months before they would have a chance to share that hilltop sight again.

The mood had lightened considerably by the time they arrived back at the house. They decided to play pictionary with the guys against the girls. They were evenly matched until the last game. The girls won, but just barely.

Just as they finished the last game, Lay and Mrs. Barry entered the house, laughing about something they had seen in the movie, they said. Mrs. Barry fixed snacks for everyone. They all carried their plates out to the porch. Lay saved a chair beside his for Mrs. Barry. No one commented on her being there, having decided it was probably a good thing and not wanting to call attention to the budding friendship.

Lay took everyone out for dinner the last evening the girls were there. Abby and Doug made a point of including Mrs. Barry in their conversations while they were there and made sure she felt welcome to go out with them on family occasions. It seemed the natural thing to do as they began accepting her into their family circle.

Witt arrived early the next morning to be on hand to see Abby and Sheryl off in Sheryl's car. Doug had suggested Abby leave her car at the ranch while she was gone.

They made plans for the next weekend. The guys insisted on being there to take them to the airport and see them off when their plane left at eight twenty-five on Sunday morning.

They all went out for breakfast Saturday morning, then spent the rest of the day at the apartment. No one felt like going anywhere. Besides, there were some last-minute details Sheryl and Abby needed to take care of. They kept telling each other it was only for two months, but it felt like it was going to be two years. Nobody wanted to go out for dinner, but the refrigerator was bare, so they called for food to be delivered.

The guys were there very early to pick up Sheryl and Abby and their luggage. They wanted to be at the airport by seven so they would have plenty of time to get checked in. Doug and Witt were allowed to accompany them only a short way before they had to say their good-byes.

After a moment's pause, Witt embraced Abby, and they shared a tender kiss, their first.

"I've wanted to do that since the first time I saw you in sixth grade." Witt smiled at her and added, "I will miss you more than you can possibly know. Have a safe trip, and may these next two months fly by."

"I will certainly miss seeing you." Abby couldn't define her feelings at that moment. She was surprised, yet she wasn't. The only thing she knew for sure was that the kiss was nice, and she wanted to repeat it as soon as possible. Now, she was really sorry to be leaving!

Doug and Sheryl's good-bye was a little more intimate—their kiss more passionate, their embrace longer as they prepared to part.

"I'm really going to miss you," Doug murmured as he reluctantly released Sheryl.

"No more than I will miss you," she whispered back to him. The guys each collected a second quick kiss from the girls before they allowed them to continue to the loading area.

Doug and Witt searched for a window where they could see the plane as it taxied. They planted themselves there, prepared to wait until they saw it take off. They both were of the same mind. It was going to be a long, lonesome two months.

On the way home, they picked up Sheryl's car so they could keep it at the ranch with Abby's so Doug could keep an eye on both of them.

CHAPTER FIVE

*I*t was midafternoon by the time Sheryl and Abby arrived at the dormitory rooms assigned to them. The rooms were on the same floor just across the hall from each other. The girls were both starved by the time they finished getting settled into their rooms, so they set out to find the campus cafeteria. After eating, they took a walk around the area to familiarize themselves with the location of some of the buildings. Sheryl found the building she would be going to, and a few minutes later, Abby spotted hers. All the buildings they were going to need were within easy walking distance of their dorm.

The next morning, they returned to the cafeteria for an early breakfast because Sheryl's sessions started at eight and continued through four o'clock with a two-hour break for lunch. Abby had two separate classes scheduled at eight-thirty and one o'clock, each one lasting three hours.

When they went to dinner that night, the girls compared notes about their day.

"The instructor explained what topics he would be covering. I think I will get a lot out of the time I'll be here. I guess there is a lot I need to learn if I'm going to take over Mrs. Jones's job. I'm really glad I came." Sheryl couldn't wait to get into her training.

"I'm going to be learning about fabrics and the proper types of dyes to use on them in the morning class. During the afternoon session, we will be discussing color combinations and types of fabrics and how to pick the right ones to complement our designs in the future. We will each have to design a dress, then pick the fabric and the color to complement that particular design for our class project. I'm so glad Carolyn suggested I come here. I know there is so much I don't know about designing. This can't help but improve my work at Margaret's." Abby was a little intimidated by how little she actually knew and how much she needed to learn about the world of fabrics and design in such a short time.

The days flew by for both Abby and Sheryl. About the only time they had to spend together was during mealtimes. On evenings, they generally had to study in connection with their classes. Both loved what they were doing and wanted to learn as much as they could while they were there.

Since there were no classes scheduled for the weekend, they spent Saturday morning catching up on their laundry at the Laundromat room located on the first floor of their building. They had planned to go shopping in the afternoon but decided they both were just too exhausted to enjoy it, so they agreed to postpone it until the next day.

They were both in Sheryl's room when Doug called her. After saying hello to her brother, Abby returned to her room to give them some privacy. She heard her phone ringing as she was unlocking the door and hurried to answer. She expected it to be her dad. He told her he would be calling while she was away.

"Hello, Dad?"

"Hi, Abby. Sorry, I'm not your dad. I hope you don't mind talking to me instead." It was Witt on the other end.

"Of course, I don't mind. It's great to hear from you. How have you been doing?" She was elated to hear his voice.

"I've missed seeing you. It seems odd to know you are half a country away. Doug said he was going to call Sheryl this evening, so I thought I'd call you. Did you have any trouble finding your dorm and getting settled in?" he asked. It was so good to hear her voice. How he wished he were there with her.

"No, it was easy to find, and it is quite comfortable. Our rooms are across the hall from each other. It's just a short walk to the buildings where we go for our classes. I'm really learning a lot about fabrics and dyes. I didn't realize just how little I know about designing. I'm truly grateful for the experience I'm getting."

"Do you go to class all day?" Witt asked.

"I have two separate classes. One is at eight-thirty, and the other is at one. They each run for three hours. We both generally have some type of homework in the evening. About the only time Sheryl and I see each other is at mealtimes. There is a cafeteria close by that has pretty good food."

"Do you have classes on Saturday and Sunday?" Witt inquired.

"No, we have the weekends free. We went to the Laundromat this morning and just took the rest of the day off. If we have the energy, I think we will probably take a taxi somewhere to do a little shopping tomorrow," Abby replied.

"Well, I won't keep you. I just wanted to know how you were getting along. If it's okay, I will call you again sometime. In the meantime, you take it easy and learn a lot while you are there." Witt bid her good-bye.

"Call me any time. It's really good to hear your voice. You take care of yourself." Abby bid him a reluctant farewell. A wave of homesickness swept over her as she heard Witt's phone disconnect. She had never been this far from home in her life. She had an urge to hear her dad's voice, so she called his number.

She felt another surge of happiness when she heard his voice.

"Hello, Dad, how are you?"

"I'm just fine. How are you getting along at your school?" Lay had been thinking about her, so he was equally glad to hear his daughter's voice.

"It's going pretty well. It seems strange to be back in school. How is Mrs. Barry getting along?"

"She's doing very well. You know her. She's always busy. I been wanting to talk to you about Agnes, er, Mrs. Barry," Lay began, then paused. "It gets lonesome sometimes around here, especially since you have been gone. She is a lot of company for me."

"It's all right, Dad. I understand." She did understand loneliness. She felt it many times after her mother had left them. She sat in her room sometimes and cried because she felt as if no one had time for her. Her dad was always busy, and her brother sometimes treated her as if she was a pest. Mrs. Barry tried to help by teaching her how to do some things around the house and showing her how to cook some simple dishes. That helped to keep her busy, and she actually enjoyed the work. At least it made her feel a little bit useful again.

"I just wanted you to know that nothing or no one can ever replace your mother. I enjoy Mrs. Barry's company, and it helps to keep the loneliness at bay for a little while when I am with her." Lay tried to explain his feelings.

"Dad, I know you loved Mother and you will always have her in your heart. I don't doubt that you are lonesome sometimes. There's nothing wrong with you finding someone who can bring you a little happiness. I think Mrs. Barry is a fine person, and if you want to keep company with her, I see nothing wrong with your doing so." Abby tried to reassure her dad that he shouldn't feel guilty for having feelings for Mrs. Barry.

"I just wanted to be sure you know I haven't forgotten your mother," Lay replied.

"Dad, it's sweet of you to be concerned about my feelings, but it's your life. Whatever makes you happy is all right with me, and I'm positive Doug will feel the same." Abby didn't tell her dad that she and Doug had already discussed the situation on more than one occasion. "Are you keeping up with your exercises that Edward left for you?" It was time to change the subject.

"Yes, my dear. If I dare skip a day, I have to answer to Agnes. Believe me, I would rather do them than be scolded by her." Lay chuckled. It was rather nice having Agnes look out after him. He missed having someone on his case if he tried to get away with something he shouldn't.

"Sounds like Mrs. Barry has you well in hand. Good for her. Tell her I said to keep it up!" Abby smiled at the thought of Mrs. Barry scolding her dad for anything. "It sounds like you are taking care of yourself, Dad, so I'll let you get back to what you were doing. I've got some reading I really should get done before I go to bed. I love you. I'll call again soon."

"I love you too, honey. You take care. Tell Sheryl hello for me." Lay, relieved to have his feelings for Agnes in the open, went in search of her as soon as he was off the phone.

Abby went back across the hall to tell Sheryl good night, but she was still deep in conversation on the phone. She assumed it was with Doug. They had all the signs of the beginnings of a serious relationship. In some ways, she envied them.

At breakfast the next morning, they were deciding what they wanted to do for the rest of the day when they were approached by two of Sheryl's classmates.

"Would you ladies mind if we joined you?" one of them asked.

"I've seen you in class. It's Sheryl, isn't it? I'm Zach, and this is Ben. Who's your friend?"

"This is Abby, but we aren't looking to meet anyone because we both have boyfriends. We're here to study and don't have much spare time," Sheryl responded.

"We're not looking for anything but friendship either. We're both from Austin, Texas, and kind of lonesome. Actually, neither of us has been to New York City. For that matter, we've never been this far from home." Ben hastened to state their intentions.

"Please, sit down," Sheryl asked the men to join them at their table.

"If you don't mind me asking, where are the two of you from?" Zach asked.

"We live in a suburb of Denver, Colorado, called Centerview. This is our first trip here also." Abby filled them in.

"Abby, what do you do? Are you taking a class here also?" Ben asked.

"I design clothing for a small dress shop. I'm here to learn something about fabrics and dyes," she responded.

"That sounds interesting. What do you ladies have planned for the rest of today?" Ben asked.

"We haven't made any plans yet. We were going to decide over breakfast." Sheryl wondered where this conversation was going. She suspected they had an ulterior motive for approaching their table.

"We heard about a bus you can catch right outside the gates that will take you on a tour of the area. They said it takes about five hours and includes lunch at a local eatery. We thought it might be something to do to pass away the day. You're both welcome if you want to join us." Zach issued the invitation.

"What do you think, Abby? Shall we go, or would you rather go shopping?" Sheryl was torn. She didn't exactly trust the guys, but they would be in public places with other people around.

"It might be interesting. We can do the shopping thing any-time." Abby thought she would rather take the bus tour. "I guess we're in. Okay?" Abby asked Sheryl.

"It's fine with me," Sheryl agreed.

"Great! The bus leaves at ten, so we'll meet you at the front gate then. We've finished our breakfast, so we'll let you get on with yours and see you later." With that, the guys left the girls to finish their meal.

"Do you think we are making a mistake?" Sheryl still wasn't at all sure they should be going with Zach and Ben.

"Well, we will be out in public all the time. What could they do with people around? It might be fun to go on this tour. If it's inter-esting, it might be something we can do with Doug and Witt if they come to see us," Abby reasoned.

The bus tour proved to be quite interesting. They saw Madison Square Garden, Lincoln Center, Rockefeller Center, and Times Square, and then they got to take a ride through Central Park, where they saw people riding horses on trails throughout the park. It was so much bigger than they expected, and greener.

Zach and Ben turned out to be good company. They both were well mannered and acted the true gentlemen. The girls were a little sorry when the tour ended. Zach invited them to accompany him and Ben to the cafeteria for something to drink before they called it a day. They readily accepted partially because they were thirsty but mostly because they had really enjoyed the day with their new friends.

Finally, it was time to return to the dorm. Zach and Ben walked the girls to the door of their building, said their good nights and then continued on to their dorm two buildings down.

"What do you think?" Abby asked as they walked up to their rooms.

"They seemed very nice, but I still feel a little guilty," Sheryl answered thoughtfully.

"Yeah, I know what you mean. I really had a nice time today, but the little voice in my head kept telling me I shouldn't be doing that," Abby agreed with Sheryl.

"It was probably just a onetime thing. I doubt that we will be doing anything like that again," Sheryl reasoned. "They're probably just as lonesome as we are."

The next morning, when they went for breakfast, they ran into Zach and Ben outside the cafeteria, where they had apparently been waiting.

"Since we all have to eat, we figured we may as well do it together." Ben greeted them as he held the door open for them to enter.

"Good morning. It's a beautiful day." Sheryl had her doubts about having breakfast with them, but so far, she had no reason to think they were up to anything. It could be that they just wanted some company.

After a quick breakfast, Zach, Ben, and Sheryl left for class. Abby stayed for another cup of coffee until it was time for her to go. She really enjoyed talking to Zach and Ben but couldn't help but wonder what Witt would think about it.

Since Sheryl's lunchtime was first, she always saved a place at a table for two, for her and Abby. Today, Zach and Ben showed up and insisted she move to a table for four so they could all eat together. She and Abby were going to have to talk about this. Something was going to have to be done about their 'shadows'.

When Ben saw Abby enter the cafeteria, he stood up and waved his arms to get her attention. When she didn't see him, he yelled her name. She heard him and waved back, looking a little embarrassed. They both rushed through lunch, anxious to get out of the cafeteria in an effort to get away from Zach and Ben for a few minutes before they had to return to class.

"What's the hurry?" Ben asked as the girls finished their lunch and rose to leave.

"We need to go back to the dorm before it's time for us to go back to class," Abby answered.

"Okay. We'll see you for dinner then?" Zach asked.

"We'll see." Sheryl avoided the question.

"What are we going to do about those two?" Sheryl asked while they walked toward their dorm in case they were being watched.

"I wish I knew. I'm afraid they're going to try to take over all of our free time." Abby sighed.

"I've enjoyed talking with them, but there is a limit to how much time I want to spend in their company." Sheryl agreed.

"I don't want to be rude, but how can we get rid of them without hurting their feelings? We are going to have to be here for another seven weeks with them." Abby was at a loss.

"We are going to have to do something! Witt and Doug definitely won't understand the situation as it is." Sheryl tried to think of a way out.

"Is there anywhere else to get food?" Abby wondered.

"I think I remember seeing some kind of a little store about a block away from the front gate. Why?" Sheryl thought that was where it was.

"We have those little refrigerators and microwave ovens in our rooms. If we have to, I guess we could fix some of our meals in our rooms and not go to the cafeteria all the time." Abby suggested an out for them.

"With our luck, they would come up here to see why we didn't show up at the cafeteria. Then they would probably invite themselves to eat with us." Sheryl chuckled.

"I expect you are right. We've got to get to school. In the meantime, let's go eat as soon as we get out of class. Maybe we can be finished by the time the guys show up," Abby suggested.

"We can only hope, but something tells me they won't be easy to get rid of," Sheryl commented as they headed out toward their classes.

As arranged, Abby and Sheryl went directly to eat as soon as they got out of class. They were on their way out of the cafeteria when they met Ben and Zach entering.

"Where are you going? It's time to eat," Zach asked.

"Come on back in with us," Ben insisted.

"We decided to eat early. Abby has some homework she needs help with." Sheryl crossed her fingers and hoped Abby would back her up.

"I took on some extra work to help in my studies," Abby explained.

"Why didn't you tell us so we could have joined you early? Now we have to eat alone, again." Ben was none too happy.

Before they returned to their rooms, the girls found the little store Sheryl had seen earlier. They were pleased to find a good supply of food items. The store clerk told them that a lot of students cooked in their dorm rooms, so the store stocked quite a cross-section of food, especially for microwaves. They would not have to return to the cafeteria again if they didn't want to.

"I guess you know this is the coward's way out," Sheryl observed after they had purchased all the supplies they could carry and were walking back to their rooms.

"I know. I feel terrible about it. I don't want to hurt their feelings. I just want them to go away. If you can think of a better plan, I'm open to suggestions." Abby wished she could think of a graceful way out for them.

"Somehow, I don't think this will solve our problem." Sheryl had a sinking feeling. "We may have to wind up telling them right out that we don't want to share every meal with them. Somehow, I don't think they are going to take rejection well."

"I know. If we make them mad, they could cause us a lot of trouble with Doug and Witt if they wanted to." That thought was unsettling to Abby.

"Oh, I hadn't thought about that!" Sheryl shuddered. "I haven't mentioned them to Doug. Have you told Witt anything about them?"

"No. I didn't mention them either. In retrospect, I guess I should have, but I had no idea they would become such a problem." Abby regretted her omission. "They might be a little hard to explain at this late date."

"We're going to have to get rid of Zach and Ben before Doug and Witt get here." Sheryl wished she knew how to go about it.

"Who would've thought we would ever have this problem, one where we have too many men?" Abby grinned at the thought.

"That's not funny." Despite her protestation, Sheryl had to smile at the situation.

"What are we going to do?" Abby asked.

"I don't know. Let's just see how it plays out the next couple of days. Maybe it won't be as bad as we think," Sheryl replied.

"I don't think we can wait. Witt mentioned something about flying in this weekend. We're going to have to do something soon, or we could very well have a couple of very unhappy boyfriends on our hands if Zach and Ben decide to show up," Abby reminded Sheryl.

"Let's talk to them at breakfast in the morning and try to explain our situation to them. Maybe they will be gentlemen about it," Sheryl suggested.

"Well, it's worth a try. At least we will have made an honest effort to end things." Abby agreed. "I guess that would be better than just trying to avoid them."

The next morning, Zach and Ben were waiting for them at the cafeteria again. As soon as they were all seated, Sheryl broached the subject foremost on her mind.

"We need to talk to both of you. Do you remember when we first met we told you we weren't looking to meet anyone because we had boyfriends?"

"Yes, but we thought you just said that in case you didn't like us," Ben answered.

"No, it wasn't that. We do have boyfriends," Abby added.

"But we all have been having a good time together! We thought you liked us!" Ben broke in.

"We had so much fun when we were on that bus tour, and then you have been eating with us all the time. You must like us because you haven't talked about your so-called boyfriends at all. If I had a girlfriend, I would be talking about her all the time. You have to be interested in us!"

"I'm sorry. We didn't intentionally lead you on. We were just trying to be friendly." Abby attempted to explain.

"It's all right. Ben." Zach understood and accepted their explanation.

"You told us that all you wanted was friendship because you were a long way from home and lonesome," Sheryl reminded Ben.

"That was just a line to get you interested. You didn't really think I meant that, did you? Everybody has a line to get a girl interested, and that was mine. It got you to go on the bus tour with us, didn't it? It got you to share all of our meals together." Ben didn't for a minute believe what the girls were saying. "If you didn't like us, you wouldn't have spent so much time in our company."

"Ben, to be fair, you were the ones insisting that we share a table for our meals, and you just wouldn't take no for an answer," Sheryl objected.

"It doesn't matter. I have invested a lot of time in you. I was going to ask you to spend this weekend doing stuff with us. You can't dump me now! I won't let you!" Ben was irate.

"Ben, forget it. It's over. They're right. I guess we did force ourselves on them. It's time to move on." Zach tried to calm his friend.

"This is not over." Ben slammed his fist down on the table, got up, and stormed off.

"I'm sorry about all this. I'll talk to him. Don't worry," Zach apologized for Ben's actions and followed his friend out.

"Well, that could have gone better." Abby had lost her appetite.

"I sure hope Zach can talk some sense into Ben." Suddenly, Sheryl wasn't hungry either.

"But what if he can't? Feeling like he does, Ben could cause us an awful lot of trouble." Now, Abby was really worried.

"I don't know about you, but I'm planning on confessing the whole mess to Doug the next time I talk to him." Sheryl dreaded it, but it would be better for him to learn it from her than have an angry Ben show up while he was here.

"I guess you're right. We had better decide exactly what we are going to tell them because as soon as we hang up, they are going to

THE DESIGNS OF LOVE

be on the phone with each other, comparing notes." Abby knew it wasn't going to be an easy conversation, but it had to be done.

"We are going to tell them the truth—how we met, the bus tour we went on with them, the meals we had with them—and why. They need to know everything we know so anything that is said here will not come as a surprise." Sheryl knew that was the way it had to be handled.

"I had better get to class, or I'll be late." Sheryl looked at her watch, surprised it was so late. She dreaded having to be in the same room with Ben as upset as he was.

"Let's eat in our rooms for a day or two. Maybe Ben will have cooled off by then," Abby suggested.

"That's a good idea. I'll see you at home. Stop by at noon, and I'll have a bite fixed for you." Sheryl waved as she headed off to class.

"Good luck!" Abby tossed over her shoulder as an afterthought when it crossed her mind that Sheryl would be spending the next three hours confined in a room with Ben.

Sheryl had sandwiches and a salad waiting for Abby by the time she arrived.

"How did your morning go?" Abby asked.

"Ben sits behind me, so I felt as if he was glaring at me all morning. I sneaked a look at him once. He looked like a thundercloud." Sheryl shivered as she remembered the look of pure hatred on his face.

"I sure hope Zach can talk some sense into him and soon." Abby felt sorry for Sheryl. She was getting the brunt of Ben's wrath. She would be facing another three hours of an angry Ben in the afternoon. It had to be wearing on her nerves.

"I'll fix dinner tonight," Abby offered. She was pretty sure Sheryl would be tired, if not stressed out, after spending another three hours in the same room as Angry Ben.

By the time Sheryl returned home, Abby had a big glass of iced tea waiting for her.

"I thought this afternoon would never end. Every time I tried to answer a question in class, I would hear a snort and a comment like 'I wouldn't trust her' or 'You can't believe a word she says'. He made sure the teacher didn't hear, but the people sitting close to us were giving us funny looks." Sheryl collapsed in the nearest chair, taking a big swallow of her tea.

By the time dinner was over, Sheryl was in a little better frame of mind. They both had some reading to do so they parted early. Sheryl couldn't help herself; she peeked out of the door to be sure no one was waiting for her when it came time for her go across the hall.

"Come over in the morning. I'll fix breakfast," Abby invited.

"Okay. That would be good. Sleep well tonight."

Angry Ben's behavior did not show any improvement over the next day.

"I'm sorry, Sheryl. I've tried to talk to Ben, but he won't listen to me. He's determined to make your life miserable," Zach apologized to Sheryl as he paused at her desk.

"What am I going to do? Do you think it would help if I apologized to him again?" Sheryl was getting desperate.

"I don't think he is in the mood to listen to anyone. I'll just keep talking to him. Maybe eventually, I'll get through to him. Right now he is a loose cannon, so I really don't know what his next move will be, but if I were you, I'd be careful," Zach cautioned.

"Do you really think he would actually harm one of us?" Sheryl hadn't thought about anything like that.

"Not physically, but I think if he got the chance, he would do his best to embarrass you." Zach tried to reassure her.

"Our boyfriends are coming on Friday night. We told them all about meeting the two of you, and they are okay with it, but I would rather they didn't meet Ben while he is still this angry with us." Sheryl tried to think what they were going to do.

"I'll see if I can keep Ben busy while they are here. He has been talking about going to the mountains. This might be a good weekend to do that," Zack offered.

"Please don't tell him the guys are coming," Sheryl asked.

"Of course not. I doubt you could blast him out of here if he knew they were going to be here. Again, I am sorry for this trouble. I had no idea he would react to the situation like he did." Zach shook his head and left quickly to intercept Ben before he saw the two of them in conversation.

Sheryl relayed her conversation with Zach to Abby. They agreed it would be better if they told no one about their weekend plans lest Ben catch wind of them. Sheryl was pretty sure they could trust Zach to keep their secret. At least, she certainly hoped they could.

Ben spent the next day in stony silence in class. When he entered each class, he stopped at Sheryl's desk and glared silently at her for ten or fifteen seconds before proceeding to his desk. She tried to apologize once, but her words were met with stony silence. From then on, she just ignored him, hoping he would get tired of that and move on.

Zach stopped by Sheryl's desk Thursday afternoon to tell her he had reservations at a cabin in the mountains. He thought he had talked Ben into going. They would catch the bus at four thirty Friday afternoon and return about six thirty Sunday evening.

"Thank you, Zach. You don't know how much I appreciate that." Sheryl breathed a sigh of relief. Maybe they could have a nice weekend after all.

At Sheryl's suggestion, Doug and Witt stopped to check in and freshen up at the motel where Abby had reserved rooms for them. It was nearly five before they arrived at the college. Sheryl had given them explicit instructions on how to find the dorm. The girls were out front, anxiously awaiting their arrival. After a joyous reunion, they were invited upstairs to see where the girls were staying.

"Let's stay here this evening. Can we just go to the cafeteria where you eat?" It had been a long day. Doug was ready to just unwind and spend time with Sheryl.

"If you want, after we eat, maybe we could take a short stroll around the campus." Abby was happy just to spend quiet time talking with Witt.

It was approaching six by the time the group arrived at the cafeteria. Even though it was well past their normal dining time, Sheryl and Abby couldn't help but glance around the room to be sure Ben wasn't there. When they didn't see him, both breathed a sigh of relief and led the guys around to get their food.

"The food is pretty good." Doug observed after tasting his food.

"Not bad," Witt agreed.

"It's okay. We discovered a little store outside the front gate, so we do some cooking in our rooms," Abby explained.

"I imagine any place would get old if you had to eat there three times a day," Witt offered.

"The exception being my house. Mrs. Barry is great!" Doug couldn't help but add.

"How are Dad and Mrs. Barry getting along?" Abby asked.

"It's weird. Dad seems to be in no hurry to take over the reins again. He is perfectly willing to help with the work when we need him, but he acts like he would rather spend time with Mrs. Barry than worry about what's going on with the ranch. I've never seen him act like this," Doug filled Abby in.

"Is he keeping up with his exercises?" Abby asked.

"Oh yeah. Mrs. Barry sees to that." Doug laughed at that.

"Did Dad talk to you about Mother?" Doug got serious again.

"Yes, he did," Abby answered.

"What do you think?" he asked.

"I know he has to have been lonesome sometimes since Mother's been gone. If he can find some solace with Mrs. Barry, then I have no problem with it," Abby slowly answered.

"The question is, how do you feel about the situation, Sheryl?" Doug asked.

"I've spent a lot of time thinking about that. If my mother can find happiness with your dad, then I have no objection to whatever happens." Sheryl gave it her blessing.

"Then we all agree. Whatever happens happens. Let them proceed at their own pace. We will all stay out of it." Doug was willing to let it go.

After finishing their meal, they took a short stroll around the campus before returning to Sheryl's room.

"Well, have you learned anything since you've been here?" Witt asked Abby.

"Yes. I'm really surprised at how little I know about fabric and dyes. And I can see your eyes glaze over when I talk about stuff like that, but I'm really happy I got to take this course. It will help me a lot down the road." Abby stopped talking about her work because she would much rather talk with Witt about more personal things, like what he had been doing while she was away.

"What about you, Sheryl? Are you learning anything?" Doug asked as he draped his arm around her shoulder.

"I'm learning a lot." She was pretty sure he didn't want to talk about her classes any more than she did. "What have you been doing in your spare time since I've been gone?" she had to ask.

"Would you believe… sitting at home, looking at your picture every night?" Doug grinned as he squeezed the back of her neck.

"No. Care to try again?" Sheryl laughed, glad to be where she was.

"Actually, we've been so busy sorting cattle and getting the hay put up that most nights I've been too tired to get into any mischief."

"What about you, Witt?" Abby asked.

"I don't have a picture of you to look at, so I've pretty much been doing what Doug has been doing—putting up hay for the winter and moving cattle around to different pastures. About all I have strength for is watching a little television," Witt answered as he walked over to stand behind Abby's chair so he could gently massage her shoulders. He just needed to be able to touch her for a few minutes.

"This weekend is sort of like a minivacation for us, isn't it, Witt?" Doug laughed.

"You got that right! My muscles have been saying 'thank you' to me all day." Witt released Abby's shoulders to rub his own.

"I hate to cut the evening short. I'm dead on my feet." Doug sighed.

"I was thinking the same thing," Witt agreed with Doug.

"I guess you both have had a long day. It's time we let you get your rest." Sheryl realized they must be worn out.

"We'll meet you at the cafeteria about eight or a little after in the morning. How would that be?" Abby asked.

"That's fine with us." Doug couldn't smother his yawn.

"Sleep well, you two, and we will see you at breakfast." Witt was well ready to get some rest.

The girls walked them to their car, and after a quick kiss, the guys were on their way. As soon as they were out of sight, the girls returned to their rooms, ready to call it a night also.

Sheryl and Abby had some suggestions for things they could do the next morning. They decided the bus tour might be the most fun. The guys had never been in this part of the country, so they wanted to see everything they could.

"It leaves at ten, so we have a few minutes before we need to be there." Abby looked at her watch. "Let's walk down to that little store so I can pick up some more batteries for my camera. I think they're getting low."

Abby and Sheryl enjoyed the tour as much as the guys did, even though it was their second time. The guys couldn't get over how big and green Central Park was. That was clearly their favorite spot of the whole tour. The park covered almost eight hundred acres of sights to see, including twenty-nine sculptures. They rode alongside a lake covering over a hundred acres. Abby had to agree with them; it was spectacular. It made her homesick for the ranch. She couldn't wait to be done with the classes so she could go home.

While they were at dinner that evening, Abby had an idea. "You know, in two weeks, it will be the Fourth of July. My instructor says we will all have four days off. Why can't we fly home then?"

"Are you sure? My instructor hasn't said anything about it." Sheryl hoped it was true.

"We talked about it in class one day. He said the school would be closed over the Fourth."

"That would be great if you can come home. I know Dad will be glad to see you." Doug liked the idea.

"He wouldn't be the only one glad to see you, Abby," Witt couldn't help but add.

"I'm sure your mother will be glad to see you also." Abby turned to Sheryl.

"Everyone will be glad to see everyone. How's that?" Doug added drily.

"Point taken," Witt answered with a smile.

"Let's find out for sure Monday and then get our tickets as soon as possible." Sheryl was anxious to find out for certain. It would certainly be nice to get away from Ben's cold stare if only for three or four days.

The plane for Denver was scheduled to leave at two o'clock, so after breakfast, the group whiled away the time in Sheryl's room, all wishing they had another day but knowing their time together had to be limited.

"Hey! Why are we so glum? Just think, in two weeks, we will be together again. That won't be so long. And when we come back, we'll be over halfway through with school." Sheryl tried to cheer everyone up.

"When you put it that way, it doesn't sound long at all." Doug felt a little better.

"I guess you are right. You two will be through with all this and back home in no time," Witt agreed, feeling a little better himself.

"Speaking of time, we had better go. By the time we stop at the motel for our stuff, we'll need to head for the airport." Doug hated to leave.

The group slowly made their way to the car. Doug and Sheryl shared a long kiss and embrace. Witt's good-bye to Abby was equally sad though not as intense. They were just at the beginning of a new relationship, and Witt didn't want to rush things with Abby just when he thought he was finally beginning to get her attention.

Abby and Sheryl stood watching the car until it was out of sight, then solemnly returned upstairs without a word until they reached their doors.

"Are you as homesick as I am?" Sheryl broke their sad silence.

"Probably more so. Do you want to come in for a while? Maybe have some coffee?" Abby was reluctant to go back into that empty room.

"Yeah, I guess. It'll beat sitting around, feeling sorry for myself." Sheryl sighed and slowly followed Abby through the door.

Monday and Angry Ben came all too soon for Sheryl. It had been nice to have a couple of days of not looking around corners to avoid him, but that was over. It was back to his angry glares and rude comments.

Abby felt sorry for her friend and what she was going through, but she didn't know of anything she could do to help her.

"We can eat here in the morning. For lunch, why don't I stop by the cafeteria and pick up sandwiches and chips? We can eat on one of the benches under a tree somewhere, out of sight of the cafeteria," Sheryl offered.

"That would be good, but it makes me feel like a coward. We can't keep running from him for the next six weeks." Abby hated to keep on avoiding Ben.

"We are not hiding from him exactly. We're just trying to avoid a confrontation in hopes Ben will cool off a little bit," Sheryl reasoned.

"Well, maybe you are right. We'll see." Abby reluctantly agreed with Sheryl.

Ben's anger hadn't lessened over the weekend. His stony silence and angry glare followed Sheryl's every move.

By Tuesday morning, Ben had heard about Witt and Doug's weekend visit.

"I hear you sneaked your boyfriends in for the weekend while I was gone. Too bad I wasn't here to greet them. We have so much in common." He stopped by her desk, waiting for her to say something.

"I don't know that you have anything in common—" Sheryl tried to answer, but she was cut off in midsentence.

"I don't want to hear any more of your lies!" Ben moved on to his seat.

Every time Ben passed Sheryl's desk, he paused to taunt her. He'd say things like 'Have you heard from your boyfriend?' or 'Did your boyfriend call you last night?' or 'Did you call your boyfriend last night?' or 'Is he a good lover?' or 'One day I will have to have a long talk with your boyfriend. When's he coming back?' Every day there was a new taunt.

At first, Sheryl attempted to respond to his comments but then decided it was best not to say anything. Maybe if she didn't respond, Ben would get tired of his sick game and move on.

After a week of Ben's harassment, he seemed to give up. He passed by Sheryl's desk in silence. She was relieved but worried that it was only a ploy, and he would start up with something else later.

The second week flew by quickly, and before they knew it, the girls were on their way home.

Doug and Witt were so anxious to see the girls that they were at the airport an hour ahead of time in case the plane was early.

Sheryl and Abby rushed into the open arms of their greeters. Doug and Sheryl's embrace was deep and passionate. Witt gave Abby a quick kiss and a big hug. She wished for more, but since he didn't offer, she withdrew.

Witt was determined to take his time with Abby. She had been first in his thoughts for what seemed like most of his life. He knew it was probably old-fashioned thinking, but he had to know that he was first in her thoughts before he dared plan a future with her. He had to know that Tyler Tracy would no longer be a factor in their relationship. He had waited this long, so he guessed it wouldn't kill him to wait a little while longer, though sometimes he had his doubts.

"We better collect our luggage before they take it to the unclaimed storeroom." Abby attempted to start toward the baggage area, but Witt stopped her progress by taking a firm grip on her hand. He had to have something! Surely, they could hold hands!

"I guess we had better go. Dad is anxious to see you, Abby, as is your mother, Sheryl." Doug agreed that it was time to go. Witt led the procession to retrieve the luggage, all the while keeping a firm grip on Abby's hand.

***

Lay and Mrs. Barry were waiting at the door to greet Abby and Sheryl. They each collected a big hug from both of them before they were allowed to pass into the house.

"Oh, how I've missed you, girl. It was bad enough having you an hour away, but now that you're halfway across the country, it's worse. Hurry up and finish your schooling so you can come back to Centerview and maybe even closer someday." Lay hadn't missed the hand-holding going on between Witt and Abby, but he chose not to comment on it for the time being. They would discuss it at a later date—of that, he had no doubt. Right now, it was enough just to know something might be happening between the two of them.

Mrs. Barry had prepared a feast the first night the girls were home. While Abby and Sheryl were helping carry dishes to the kitchen, Mrs. Barry caught Abby alone for a moment.

"I know your father talked to you about us. I just want you to know I would never try to take your sainted mother's place. I am just trying to make a little space of my own in your lives. It would make me very happy if you could see fit to call me Agnes."

"I will be very pleased to call you Agnes. I know you make my father happy, so I will be very glad to welcome you into our family." Abby gave Agnes a quick hug as Sheryl came in with another armful of dishes from the dining room. After the kitchen work was finished, they all spent the evening catching the girls up on some of the things they had missed out on. Abby would have liked to have asked about Tyler but decided this was not the time to bring up that subject. Maybe later she would have a chance to talk to her dad about him.

Lay decreed that everyone have an early night to give the girls a chance to rest up from their travel. Tomorrow was the Fourth, and he had plans for everyone to attend the fireworks show put on every year by the city of Everett, so they would be up late for that.

Saturday morning was warm and bright as they all gathered for the morning meal. After breakfast, Witt took the girls and Doug for a visit with his parents. He took with him an invitation to a family barbecue at Lay's on Sunday evening. They readily accepted the offer, and Witt's mother asked Sheryl to tell her mother she would be calling to see what she could do to help out.

After having lunch there, they returned home, where Doug took them a quick tour of the Andrews ranch. By the time they got back it was nearly dinnertime. Earlier in the day, Lay had called Hank to see if he and Elizabeth wanted to ride with them into town. As soon as they arrived, everyone divided up into two cars. Lay, Agnes, Hank, and Elizabeth led off, and Doug, Sheryl, Witt, and Abby followed in Doug's car.

The weather was picture-perfect as the backdrop for the fireworks show. Abby had attended the fireworks shows since she could remember, but she didn't think she had ever enjoyed the show more. The fact that she was leaning comfortably back against Witt with his arms draped loosely around her shoulders certainly helped.

Sheryl looked quite comfortable snuggled up against Doug, his arms firmly wrapped around her. She didn't see her dad and Agnes but assumed they were just as comfortable wherever they were.

It was nearing midnight by the time they got out of the park and arrived home. It had been a long day, so everyone was ready to say their good nights and go to bed in short order.

Sunday was mostly spent preparing for the party. Agnes sent Sheryl and Abby into town with a list of things she was going to need. Doug and Witt were busy putting up the canopy over the patio and setting up the tables under it so they would be in the shade. After that, Lay took command of the kitchen for a short while as he directed them on how to make the marinade to use in preparing the meat to be put on the grill at the proper time.

One thing Doug really wanted to do was go to the hill to watch the sun go down while Sheryl was there. He told Witt what he had in mind, and Witt made sure the girls were there at the appointed time. Thirty minutes before sundown, they piled into the ATV and headed for their special spot on the hill.

When they had been there previously, the sun was the backdrop to the valley below. Now it was ending its day's journey behind a mountain peak. Its shadows gave rise to towering purple and umber cliffs that, for a short time, gave the illusion that the mountain was on fire. As the sun settled behind the mountain's crest, the flames faded into a bed of coals, its embers slowly dying as the quiet of darkness settled over the area.

No one uttered a word as the sun disappeared into the horizon. It was as if the sight they had just witnessed cast a spell on the group, and no one was in a hurry to break it.

Finally, a full ten minutes after the sun disappeared, Witt suggested they get back before Lay sent out a search party for them. They were all laughing as they pulled up at the edge of the yard, apologetic for being late. Hank and Elizabeth had already arrived on the scene. Lay, with Hank's help, was overseeing the final preparation of the meats, and Agnes, along with Elizabeth, was preparing the tables. The girls immediately began to help carry things out of the house for the tables, and the guys relieved Lay and Hank of the meat preparation, relegating them to advisors and official tasters.

Between the citronella candles resting on the tables, which were covered with brightly colored clothes, and the tiki torches placed strategically around the canopy, the patio looked quite festive. In due time, all the preparations were completed, and it was time to eat. It was an evening full of laughter and high spirits. After everyone had eaten their fill and the food put away, someone suggested they clear off one end of the patio for dancing. Lay put on some music and started it off by asking Agnes to join him, immediately followed by the rest of the group.

It was nearing midnight when Hank suggested it was time to call it a night because the girls were going to have to get up early the next morning to catch their plane back to school.

It was a quiet ride to the airport the next morning, and in due time, Doug and Witt bid the girls a reluctant farewell with a promise to see them in two weeks. As they had done earlier, they found the window to watch the plane as it left the airport. The car seemed so lonely on the way home.

**

By late evening, the girls arrived back at their dorm rooms.

Sheryl dreaded the start of her class and seeing Ben again. She was sure that by then he had heard about their trip back to Colorado for the weekend and would have a new round of insults for her.

However, he made no comment as he passed her desk. In fact, he ignored her completely. After a couple of days, she began to relax a little because she was beginning to believe Ben's wrath had run its course and he had moved on.

They returned to the cafeteria for their meals with no incidents. Abby saw Zach and Ben sharing a table with two other girls once, so she fervently hoped they could finally put their experience in the past.

The days passed quickly, and then it was time for Doug and Witt to spend the weekend. Sheryl reserved the same motel rooms for them, and the girls hurried home from class so they could get ready and be downstairs to greet the guys when they finally got there.

After a joyous reunion, they all went upstairs to decide where to have dinner. Doug remembered seeing a restaurant a couple of blocks from their motel. They went there for their evening meal and took a short walk around the campus afterwards to walk off their dinner before returning to the dorm rooms.

Everyone was reluctant to say good night, but finally, they parted with a plan to meet at the cafeteria for breakfast the next morning.

Sheryl spotted Ben sitting at a table across the room when they first went in. She immediately had a premonition that he was going to cause trouble for her if he could.

As soon they all got their food and sat down, Ben stood up. Sheryl and Abby were facing him as he approached their table. There was no time to warn Doug or Witt before he stopped at the end of their table, hands on hips.

"You must be the illustrious boyfriend from Colorado," he demanded, glaring at Doug.

"I must be." Doug laid his fork down as he calmly looked up at Ben.

"Did she tell you we had a pretty good thing going before you decided to show up?" Ben asked with a sneer.

"She did," Doug answered.

"Did she tell you we spent the entire day together once?" he asked.

"She did. I believe it was also with Abby and a busload of tourists." Doug answered Ben's questions calmly.

"Did she tell you we had been sharing all of our meals and walking to class together before you decided to come here?"

"She did. I understand it was at your insistence. She was perfectly happy sharing a table for two with Abby before you stepped in," Doug added. "If I'm not mistaken, both ladies also told you the first time you spoke to them that they had gentlemen friends and were not interested in a relationship other than friendship."

"Women always say something like that, but it is just a line to get someone like me interested in them." The conversation wasn't going the way Ben expected. "I think it's time for Sheryl to make a choice between you and me. Given the chance, I can make her very happy. I come from a very wealthy family in Texas, so she could have anything she wants with me. What can you offer to top that?" he demanded.

"This not a competition." Doug was struggling to stay calm by now.

"Go on. Ask her which one of us she prefers," Ben demanded.

"No."

"What do you mean no?" Ben didn't expect that.

"No gentleman would ever ask a lady a question like that." Doug leveled an icy stare at Ben.

"It's a simple question. All she needs to do is to say whether it's you or me. What's so difficult about that?" Ben was beginning to become agitated.

"A decision like that should take a great deal of thought. One should never rush into things that will affect the rest of one's life." Doug willed himself not to react to Ben's taunts.

"Maybe we had better step outside and settle this strictly between us. Winner take all!" Ben was getting desperate.

"No." Doug didn't blink an eye.

"Are you afraid to?" Ben dared Doug.

"I won't stoop to anything as crude as that." Doug refused Ben's offer.

"It seems to me that would solve everything." Ben was perplexed.

"How would it possibly help this situation at all?" Doug had regained his calm.

"It would certainly make me feel better if I got to beat you to a pulp. That's the situation it would help." Ben renewed his dare.

Doug's patience had reached its limit. He laid his napkin carefully beside his plate and slowly slid his chair away from the table.

No one at the table could breathe as they watched Doug rise to face his adversary. Ben took a step back when he saw the cold glint in Doug's eyes.

Doug took a step forward so he could be inches from Ben's face.

"Look, Ben whatever-your-last-name is, I'll tell you what I will do though, if you dare speak a word to Sheryl or Abby ever again." Doug jabbed Ben's chest with his finger to be sure he had his full attention. "I will gladly come back here and take you apart limb by limb, pack you and your limbs in dry ice, and send the box to Texas for your wealthy family to reassemble. Now, that is not a threat. It is a promise. Is that clear enough for you?" Doug stepped back a bit and looked down at his plate. "Now why don't you just run along? My breakfast is getting cold." With a wave of his hand, Doug dismissed Ben.

Ben didn't utter another word. He just turned and walked away, totally defeated.

Doug sat back down to utter silence because his table companions were still speechless.

"That was impressive." Witt was the first to regain his voice.

"I may need to sit here a while. I don't think my legs will work again until I can get my knees to quit knocking." Doug mustered a weak smile as he took a drink of his coffee in an effort to get his emotions back under control.

"Thank you, Doug." Sheryl reached across the table to take hold of Doug's hand. "You may have just made our lives a lot simpler for the last two weeks we are here."

"Hey! It is only two weeks! The next time we see each other, you will both be home for good!" Witt would be very thankful to have Abby closer. Now that he was getting her attention, he didn't want to waste any more time.

***

Sheryl couldn't help but be a little nervous as she went to class on Monday. But evidently, Doug's words must have made an impression, for Ben gave her desk a wide berth.

The girls returned to the cafeteria for all their meals. If Ben showed up at all, he made sure to sit on the opposite side of the dining room.

Zach stopped by their table one morning. "Someone told me that Ben had a confrontation with your gentleman friend while he was here over the weekend. I understand he was definitely not the winner. I just wanted you to know how sorry I am for the whole business. I didn't know Ben before we came here even though we work at the same place. I have no intention of continuing a friendship with him when we return to Texas. Again, I'm so very sorry about everything that happened."

"You have nothing to be sorry about, Zach. You tried to stop him, but clearly he was out of control from the beginning. I doubt that anyone could have done anything to prevent it." Sheryl appreciated his words of apology but thought them unnecessary.

"It sounds like you have a good man, Sheryl. You should hang on to him." He grinned, tilted his head and raised an eyebrow, leading the girls to suspect that he knew the whole story of what went on and approved of it. "I'll leave you ladies with your breakfast. Have a good day." He bowed slightly and walked away.

"Now, there goes a very nice man," Sheryl commented as they watched Zach make his way out of the dining room.

The last week was full of tests and last-minute details. Abby's group had to turn in their designs, fabric swatches, and color choices no later than Friday of the week before the last week, so Abby had to burn the midnight oil to complete her project besides keeping up to the day-to-day class assignments.

Sheryl had to do extra work on assignments due the last week also, so the girls frequently skipped their evening meal and ate whatever they could find in their refrigerators.

The last week in Abby's class was devoted to the students critiquing their classmates' projects. People generally had good things to say about most of the designs. On occasion, they didn't like the combination of color or fabric chosen to accompany the design. When it came to Abby's project, no one found fault with any of her choices. The instructor asked her to stay after class on Friday.

"Seldom do we see a student with the natural eye you seem to have for clothing design and color combination. We always show what we consider to be the best designs from each session to what is arguably the top fashion house located in New York City. They were very impressed with what they saw in your work. They would very much like to talk to you." Her instructor passed on the information to Abby.

"I don't know. I have a job waiting for me at home. I like what I am doing there." Abby was thrilled at the offer, but she had promised Carolyn she would return.

"Would you at least go talk to them? See what they have to offer. I will call and set up an appointment for you the first of the week." If only Abby would look at the operation, the instructor thought she might change her mind.

"I have plane tickets to go home tomorrow." Abby really didn't want to delay her return home to Witt.

"I'll tell you what. How about a trip back here later? They really want to talk to you, so I'm sure they will pay all the expenses just to get to you back for an interview, with no strings attached. Any time you want. You can set the date. I'll give them your information, and I expect they will be contacting you within the next week or two."

"I guess it wouldn't hurt to talk to them and see what they offer." It would give her a chance to see what a real fashion house looked like and how it worked. Abby had to admit she was intrigued, but there was no way she was going to take a job there. This last two months were as long as she ever wanted to be away from home again. Still, if there were no strings attached, it wouldn't hurt to look.

Everyone received grade cards on the last day. Abby finished at the top of her class.

Sheryl tied with another student for top honors in her class.

Both girls were exuberant that they had done so well, but they were even happier to be going home the next day.

Abby related to Sheryl the request made by The Fashion House.

"Would you take a job there if they offered it?" Sheryl knew it could be the beginning of a great career for her friend. She also knew how much family and home meant to Abby. That would be a hard decision to make, but Sheryl thought she knew Abby well enough to know she would ultimately decide to stay in Colorado.

"I have to admit, part of me wants to go talk to them, but the rest of me realizes I will be better off in Centerview, closer to home. I'm happy there, so why shouldn't I stay where I'm happy?" Abby was torn. She knew this could be a big break for her. She also knew she was going to have to do a lot of thinking before she came to a decision of this magnitude.

***

Doug and Witt were waiting at the gate, each with a dozen roses, to meet the girls. Doug picked Sheryl up in a bear hug and swung her around in pure glee. Witt and Abby embraced and kissed, gently at first, then something awoke within the both of them, and the kiss deepened, as did their hold on each other. It was as if they were the only two people in the world and time was standing still. Finally, they became aware of their surroundings and reluctantly pulled apart, each a bit dazed. They found Doug and Sheryl watching them, each with an 'I told you so' expression on their face.

Embarrassed, Abby suggested they pick up the baggage and get started home. They led the way to the luggage carousel, their hands tightly clasped together.

Doug and Sheryl smiled at each other but made no comment at what they had just seen as they followed the other two down the stairs.

When they arrived home, Lay had champagne waiting for them. He also had news of his own. He had asked Agnes to marry him, and she accepted.

It was hugs for everyone as they celebrated the engagement. Doug, Abby, Witt, and Sheryl each offered a toast to the happy couple.

Agnes had prepared sandwiches and finger foods for a light lunch for the group. Abby and Sheryl insisted that they be allowed to take care of the food while she joined everyone else on the front porch.

"So have you set the date yet?" Abby asked as soon as they all had filled their plates and sat down to eat.

"No, this just happened last night, so we haven't discussed it yet, but we're in no hurry," Lay answered as he reached for Agnes's hand to show off the ring he had given her. Agnes blushed as she let them all take turns admiring her new ring.

"I told him I didn't need a ring because I'm too old for such a thing, but he insisted."

"You never get too old for jewelry, especially an engagement ring and certainly not when it's this beautiful." Sheryl was the first to see it. Everybody else echoed her sentiment.

"I just thought of something. This will make us sisters," Sheryl commented.

"I think that's a great idea," Abby added.

"We've been practically that for a long time, now it will be official." Sheryl liked the idea.

It was so pleasant on the porch that no one wanted to break up the group, but finally, Lay caught Sheryl yawning, so he declared it nap time for the girls.

After a couple of hours of rest, the girls came downstairs to a busy house. Hank and Elizabeth had been invited over for an impromptu dinner that evening. They found Agnes busy at work in the kitchen.

"Agnes, you are practically family now. In this family, everyone pitches in to help," Abby insisted after Agnes told them to go out on the porch and rest because she had things well under control.

"We're here. Now let us help. Tell us what you need us to do, and we'll do our best to get it done." Sheryl agreed with Abby.

"You girls are going to spoil me." Agnes wrapped an arm around each girl and hugged them tightly before she released them.

"Just keep in mind that you are no longer the housekeeper. You are family. You don't have to do it all. We're here to help when we can," Abby reminded her.

"We're really good at doing as we're told. Well, most of the time, we are," Sheryl chimed in.

"I'll try to remember that, but this is all so new to me," Agnes promised. "In the meantime, I need someone to check the glasses for spots and the silverware to see if it will need to be polished."

"That didn't take long." Sheryl gave her mother a kiss on the cheek as the girls prepared to pitch in and do their part.

The evening was filled with good food and laughter with young love everywhere. It ended the same as the last time the families got together—dancing on the patio. Again Lay and Agnes led off, this time with his favorite waltz, and everyone else soon followed suit. It was nearly midnight before the party broke up.

The girls slept late Sunday morning. By the time they came downstairs, everyone else had eaten and begun their work for the day. They apologized to Agnes for being so late when they found her in the kitchen, keeping breakfast warm for them.

"We thought it would do you both good to sleep in this morning, it being your first day back and all." Agnes happily accepted a peck on the cheek from both of the girls as she fixed a breakfast plate for each of them.

"You make the best coffee in the world, Mom." Sheryl emptied her first cup and went back for a refill.

"I'll second that," Abby agreed as she held her cup out for a refill, too comfortable to move if she didn't have to.

"What do you want to do today?" Sheryl asked.

"I don't know. Let's go out on the porch and talk it over. Can we do anything to help out in here, Agnes?" Abby asked. That might be a good place to start.

"I don't know of anything right now. I think your dad is already out there. Here, would you take these sweet rolls with you? He likes one with coffee about midmorning. Tell him I'll be out in few minutes with the coffee."

Sheryl kept waiting for Abby to bring up the subject of the Fashion House offer, but since she didn't, Sheryl held her tongue. Maybe Abby was trying to make up her own mind before she brought the subject up to everyone.

"When do you think we should go to the apartment?" Abby hated to bring up the subject, but they needed to decide. Both of them had Monday off, so they could put the trip off until the next day. It was going to take a little while to stock up on things they would need.

"I guess we should probably go in the morning. Then we would have time to get restocked." Sheryl was so comfortable she would have said anything to put off the trip until tomorrow.

"Sounds like a plan. That way, we can have the whole day here to relax." That suited Abby just fine.

Another trip to their special spot on the hill was planned, but clouds rolled in to cancel their plans. A gentle rain moved in, so everyone moved to the front porch to spend the evening and enjoy the cool air the rain had brought in. Someone suggested a game of charades. Lay and Agnes opted to stay on the porch, but the rest of them moved inside. After a couple of hours, the guys were up one game. They were ready to quit while they were ahead, but the girls insisted on one more game. The girls won it, so it was necessary to have one more to break the tie. Sure enough, the guys lost again.

"We got to come up with something we can win at." Doug looked at Witt, more than a little chagrined at yet another loss to the girls.

"Yeah. But what?" Witt shook his head, at a loss. They hadn't won a single contest from the girls so far.

"There has to be something that we are better at. We just have to figure out what the heck it is," Doug insisted.

"We may have to accept the fact that the only way we are ever going to be able to beat them is to infiltrate their minds and see if we can figure out how their brains operate," Witt mused glumly.

"Do you think that would work?" Doug asked.

"No. But won't we have fun while we are trying to find out if it will?" Witt winked at Doug.

"Oh, yeah," Doug agreed.

CHAPTER SIX

*S*ince the girls had left their cars at the ranch for Doug to keep an eye on and start them once in a while to keep the batteries up while they were gone, all they had to do on Monday was pack them up and head for their apartment.

With everyone's help, their cars were loaded quickly, and it was soon time for them to say their good-byes. Doug and Witt promised to see them the next weekend. Agnes packed a lunch for them because she knew there would be nothing in the refrigerator when they got home. They promised to be careful on the road and to call home as soon as they got to the apartment. Having done that, they went to the store to restock their cupboards while the air conditioner was cooling the apartment. By evening, they were pretty much settled in and ready to go to work the next day. In a way, they were both really looking forward to getting back to their daily routine.

The Fashion House was never far from Abby's thoughts. Oh, how she would have loved to have been able to seriously consider a job there. But there was her promise to Carolyn to return to Margaret's and then, more importantly, there was Witt. She knew their relationship was certainly more than just friendship now, but she wanted to give it a chance to see where they were headed. She certainly didn't want to ever be that far away from him again. Those last eight weeks were enough. There was only one thing she could do. She was going to have to put her feelings aside because the reasons to stay were more compelling than the ones to go. Carolyn was depending on her to return, and she couldn't go back on her word.

Carolyn and Margaret insisted on hearing all about her experiences at the college when she went back to the store the next day. Work at the store had been going very well. Carolyn loved being able to work with people. A couple of her clients were so pleased with her work that they had come back to have her make a second dress. Margaret was thrilled to have this time with her daughter. She was really going to miss Carolyn when she returned to the city.

Abby put aside her New York City dreams and set about resuming the work she had been doing all along.

"I guess you will be glad to get out of here, won't you?" she commented to Carolyn.

"I probably should finish the projects I've started, and then I will be out of your hair. I need to start looking for a job." Carolyn avoided the question and instead explained her plans.

"I expect you should finish them. The clients probably wouldn't like it if we switched in the middle of an order," Abby agreed. "Are you going to try to find work at another style house in the city?"

"I don't think so. I really like working with people, so I think I will try to find a small shop similar to this one." Carolyn was starting to rethink going to New York City, but she had given her word to Abby. "Did you pick up any new tricks at your training session? As I recall, they gave us a great deal of information, but I didn't get to use what I learned for a while, so I have forgotten most of the stuff I picked up."

"I loved every moment of it. I learned a lot that I will be able to use here every day. It was well worth the time it took." Abby had no regrets in taking the training session because she learned so many new things that could only help her. "I imagine you would find it very useful if you could take it again before you looked for another job."

"I've been thinking about enrolling in it again. I guess it might be a good idea to take a refresher course and now would be the time to go." Carolyn was going to seriously think about it.

Carolyn was putting the last touches on her final client's dress when Mrs. McDaniels, her first client at the shop, returned, asking for her.

"Do you remember when I had you make a dress for my grand-daughter's wedding about three months ago?" she asked Carolyn.

"Yes, I'll never forget it. Yours was my very first attempt at a dress after I started here. How did the wedding turn out? I'll bet it was beautiful." Carolyn recalled the experience with ease. "How can we help you now?"

"It was absolutely perfect. Now I have a second granddaughter who has decided to get married, so I need you to make me another dress," Mrs. McDaniels responded.

"Oh, I'm sorry, Carolyn. I forgot my manners. This is my grandson, Carter. He is driving me around today. It's his sister who's getting married." She laid her hand on Carter's arm as she introduced him to Carolyn.

"It's nice to meet you, Carter." Carolyn shook the young man's hand.

"How do you do, Carolyn? It's very nice to meet you." Carter returned the greeting. He couldn't help but notice how attractive the young seamstress was.

"I'll give all your measurements to Abby. She will be helping you with your new dress. I'm planning on going back to New York City in a few days." Carolyn prepared to turn her over to Abby.

"Oh, please. Can't you stay and make my new dress yourself? I mean no offense to the other girl, but you did such a beautiful job on that first dress," Mrs. McDaniels pleaded.

"What do you think, Abby?" Carolyn asked.

"I think if Mrs. McDaniels wants you, she most certainly should have you." Abby laughingly answered her friend's query.

"You won't mind me staying a few more days?" Carolyn wanted to be sure.

"It's fine with me." Abby went back to what she had been doing, leaving Carolyn to deal with her client.

***

The answering machine was blinking when Abby got home that evening. It was a call from the Fashion House.

"Miss Andrews, this is Sylvia Standfield of the Fashion House. I would like very much to speak with you. Could you return my call at your convenience? It's important."

Just as she thought, she had put that subject behind her. It had become foremost in her thoughts again! What was she going to do? Her first thought was to ignore the call, but she knew she couldn't in good conscience do that. She had to reply to the message.

She punched in the phone number and asked for Miss Standfield. A moment later, her call was put through.

"Miss Andrews? I'm sorry it took so long to contact you. I've been looking at the designs you did for that training session, and I must say that I am very impressed. Tell me, how much formal training have you had in the field of design?"

"Actually, none. I started making my own clothes while I was in grade school. I used ready-made patterns at first, then started to modify them to suit my own taste. By the time I was in high school, I was designing my own clothes and for some of my friends. Right now, I am working in a small dress shop, designing dresses for its clients."

"Do you mean to tell me you picked all of this up on your own?" Sylvia had heard of natural talent, but this was her first experience with it.

"Yes. That training session in New York City is the first one I have ever attended. I was amazed at how much I didn't know about fabrics and dyes," Abby admitted.

"Natural talent is a rare thing. I would love to talk with you about it. Could you possibly come visit us? You set the time, and we will take care of everything."

"While I would love to see how the Fashion House does things, I'm afraid I would be wasting your time and money." Oh, what she wouldn't give to be able to accept the offer.

"You let us worry about that. If you will come, even for two or three days, we'll meet you at the airport. We'll have a hotel suite reserved for you and a car and driver at your disposal while you are here. All we ask is a little of your time. There will be no strings attached. In the end, the decision is completely yours."

Abby was sorely tempted to accept the offer. Thanks to Mrs. McDaniels, Carolyn was going to be there for a while longer. She really would like to see how the professionals did it. "Well, as long as I'm not committing to anything, I really would like to see how your operation works. I could leave here next Monday morning. If you're sure it is all right." Abby agreed to make the trip.

"Wonderful! I will make all the arrangements and contact you later." Sylvia was elated to get Abby to agree to go there.

"That will be fine, Miss Standfield. Good evening."

"I'll be talking to you again soon. Thank you. Good night."

When Sheryl got home, Abby told her about her conversation with Miss Standfield.

"I'm glad you are going. If you don't, you will always wonder if you made a mistake. This way, you can make an informed decision. Who knows, this could be the break of your lifetime. You have to think about your future. With the talent you have, you could have a wonderful career working with professionals."

"But what about Witt?" Abby asked.

"Witt will always want what's best for you. In your heart, you know that. He would never stand in your way. You need to tell him before you go though," Sheryl reminded Abby.

"I know. I'll try to explain where I'm going and why to Witt this weekend. I'm so confused. I don't even know for sure where Witt and I are." Abby sighed and sank down in the nearest chair. "I need more time to figure out where we're headed."

"I know this is a tough spot to be in. It has to come down to what is most important to you. You can't make a snap decision. Wait until you see what they have to offer. Perhaps that will make your decision easier." Sheryl wished she could help her friend, but it was all up to Abby. The choice she made now would affect the rest of her life.

The next morning, Abby tried to explain to Margaret and Carolyn about the phone call.

"I'm sorry I haven't mentioned this earlier, but I honestly thought the subject was closed and I would be staying here. Then when Miss Standfield from the Fashion House called last night, it just opened everything back up again."

"Did you say the Fashion House?" Carolyn asked.

"Yes. When my instructor first told me about them wanting to talk to me, she mentioned the name the Fashion House, and she also said they were one of the best in New York City," Abby answered. "They wanted to talk to me right then, but I put them off because I wanted to get back home. The instructor said they would be contacting me later. I really didn't think they would actually call me."

"The Fashion House was where I went to work after college. I think you should go look around. Their operation will impress you. The only advice I will give you is, if you come across a good-looking rat named Jeffery, turn around and run away!" Carolyn could laugh about her experience now. Her conversations with Abby helped her to put what happened to her in perspective.

Mrs. McDaniel's grandson, Carter, dropped by the shop one day to ask Carolyn if he could take her to lunch. She liked him immediately, so she was happy to accept when he asked her out for dinner and a movie on Saturday evening. She found him to be very good company, so for the time being, she was in no hurry to go back to the city.

"Are you sure he's not married?" Abby couldn't resist the temptation to ask the question when she heard about their date.

"Absolutely! I checked with his grandmother. I don't think Granny would fib to me." Carolyn laughed as she answered.

Abby dreaded telling Witt about her trip, but she had to know how he felt about the situation. If he asked her to stay, that was what she would do. Part of her hoped he would indeed ask her not to go, but her curiosity made her want to see how a big company like that was operated.

The guys arrived in time for dinner Friday evening. They ate at a nearby restaurant and then returned to the apartment to spend the evening. After they had been home a few minutes, Sheryl asked Doug to walk down to her car with her to get something she had forgotten.

On the way, she explained to Doug what was going on with Abby and her job offer.

"I thought they needed some privacy so she can talk to Witt about it. You don't mind if we stay down here for a little while, do you?" She wrapped her arm around his waist.

"Of course not, I'm all in favor of anything that will get me a little time alone with you." Doug grinned and wrapped his arms around her. "That poor kid. This could be her big break. But in order to take it, she will have to give Witt up just when it's beginning to look like they're getting serious."

"That's just it. She doesn't know where she stands with him. Every time she thinks they are getting close, he seems to back off a little, and she doesn't understand why," Sheryl explained.

"I've noticed that too. I think he's trying to take his time and not rush her. He wants her to be sure." Doug thought that was probably the reason. "I know for a fact that he's crazy about her and has been for years."

"Witt is the one I feel sorry for. Doug, you know as well as I do that he would never stand in the way of something that would help Abby. But it'll break his heart if he has to let her go." Sheryl felt utterly helpless about the situation.

Meanwhile, upstairs Abby was trying to explain to Witt about the Fashion House and the interest they had shown in her. Witt sat quietly while she apologized for not telling him sooner about the job offer and about the phone call she had received a few days earlier from Miss Standfield.

"Is this something you want to do?" He had to ask the question.

"I don't know," Abby answered. "I thought I had made up my mind to stay here. Then Miss Standfield phoned me. She offered to pay all my expenses if I would just go talk to them, no strings attached. I guess they really want to see me. I don't know what to do."

"You do know you have to go talk with them, don't you? If you don't, you will always wonder whether you made the right decision or not." That was the last piece of advice he wanted to give her, but he knew it was the right thing to do.

"If you want me to stay here, I will cancel the trip in a minute."
Part of her hoped he would.

"I can't help you make a decision like that. You have to know
how I feel about you, but you are going to have to decide what is best
for you at this time in your life." He moved to stand in front of the
chair in which she was seated, gently pulled her up, wrapped his arms
tightly around her, and just held her, trying in his own way to give
her the strength to make the right decision—for herself and for him.

Darkness was settling in when Doug and Sheryl returned to the
apartment. Witt and Abby were sitting on the sofa, eating ice cream.

"Everything all right up here?" Sheryl dared to ask.

"We've been better. But it's okay," Witt quietly answered for
the both of them. "Abby is going to New York City for a few days
next week. In the meantime, we have the rest of the weekend to
enjoy. What would you two think about a tour of the capitol building tomorrow and maybe a dinner theater tomorrow evening?"

"That sounds good to me. Is there any ice cream left, or did you
guys take it all?" Doug was glad to talk about something else.

"I think there might be a little left." Abby answered. "We left
you a cookie apiece though."

"Gee, thanks." Doug got the last cookies out of the cookie jar,
while Sheryl dished up the remainder of the ice cream.

"Is there anything good on TV tonight?" Doug asked as he
picked up the TV guide and started thumbing through it, looking
for the Friday schedule. "I see there's a new comedy movie coming
on next. Is that all right with everybody?"

The guys picked Sheryl and Abby up early the next morning for
breakfast at the local smorgasbord near where they lived.

Witt and Abby seemed determined to make this a fun day for
everyone, so Doug and Sheryl went along with them even though
sometimes their laughter was a little forced.

None of them had been to the capitol since their grade school
field trip days, so they found it very interesting. Sheryl made reservations for the dinner theater that evening. It was a light musical comedy enjoyed by all. They all were actually in a better frame of mind
when they left the theater than they had been all day.

After a few minutes to say their good nights, the group called it an evening, agreeing to go back to the smorgasbord for breakfast the next morning.

They couldn't think of anything they all wanted to do the next day so they opted to go to a movie near the apartment.

By the time the movie was out and they had eaten an early dinner, it was time for the guys to leave. Witt asked Abby to call him when she got back from her trip, and she promised she would. Doug offered to catch their dad up on what was happening with Abby.

"Thanks, but I guess I had better talk to him. I'll call him in a little while." This whole thing was getting so complicated. Why didn't she just turn those people down in the beginning? Her life would be so much simpler if she had.

Her conversation with her dad was a little easier than it had been with Witt.

"What would you do at that place in New York City that you can't do here?" he asked after she explained what was going on.

"I don't know if I would be doing anything different either place. I would guess I will not be dealing with people as much there." She had not considered that.

"Would you still be designing dresses there?" Lay asked.

"Yes, I imagine so. The difference probably would be that I would just design clothing. I don't think they will be for anyone special," Abby answered.

"Do you like it when you see your design on the person you have made it for?"

"Yes. I get a thrill out of taking a blank piece of paper and watching what I draw on that paper becomes a beautiful dress for someone." It was another thing she hadn't thought about.

"I think you need to go to New York City to look around at what they have to offer. Ask a lot of questions and listen closely to their answers. Sometimes what a person doesn't say is as important as what they do say. Don't make any decisions while you are there." Lay gave her the best advice he could come up with. "Ultimately, the decision you make must be made by you, and it must be what you think is best for you."

126

"Thanks, Dad. I can see I need to do a lot more thinking before I will be able to figure things out and know what I want to do. I love you, and I'll call you soon. Tell Agnes hello for me and give her my love. Good-bye."

"Goodnight, Daughter. I've no doubt you will make the best decision for you."

***

Nine o'clock Monday morning found a very nervous Abby at the airport, waiting to get on the ten o'clock flight to New York City.

A uniformed man holding a sign with her name on it was waiting when she arrived there. In no time, he gathered her luggage and delivered her to a suite in a very upscale hotel. He set her luggage just inside its door, and then bid her good afternoon, promising to be downstairs the next morning, waiting to drive her to the Fashion House.

"What time should I come down?" Abby asked before he closed the door.

"Someone will call you, Miss."

Abby looked around the room. Actually, she had two rooms and a huge bathroom with a Jacuzzi in it. She had just finished hanging up the last of the outfits she brought with her when her telephone rang.

"Miss Andrews?" a voice on the line inquired.

"Yes," Abby answered.

"This is Clara, Miss Standfield's assistant. She is going to be tied up in meetings for the rest of the day, so she asked me to welcome you to New York City. She has cleared her calendar for tomorrow, so she will be free to show you around. She was wondering if you could be here about ten in the morning," she asked.

"Yes, I can be there. How do I get in touch with my driver, so I can tell him when to pick me up?" Abby asked.

"I'll take care of that. You just be in the lobby in the morning by nine forty-five, and he will be there. Do you have any more questions?"

"Where is the nearest restaurant?" Abby realized she was going to need to eat pretty soon.

"There is a very nice restaurant just off the lobby in your hotel. Just charge your meals to your room." Clara explained. "Is there anything else?"

"No, I think that will do it. Thank you," Abby replied.

"Good day, Miss Andrews. I expect I will see you tomorrow." Clara ended the phone call.

"Good-bye," Abby replied just as the phone went dead.

Abby had never been in a Jacuzzi, so she was anxious to try it out, but she decided first things first, and went downstairs in search of the restaurant.

It had a small coffee shop on one side and a formal dining room on the other. She opted for the smaller area with a more casual atmosphere.

The food was superb, and soon she had her fill. The next stop was going to be the Jacuzzi for a long soak, if that was what you did in them.

After a surprisingly good night's sleep, she had an early breakfast and was in the lobby before nine thirty in anticipation of her day with Miss Standfield.

Her driver escorted her to Miss Standfield's office, bid her a good day, and disappeared, leaving her in the capable hands of Clara.

"Good morning. Miss Standfield will be out as soon as she completes her phone call. Please have a seat. May I get you something to drink while you are waiting?" Clara greeted her.

"No, I'm fine. Thank you." Abby couldn't help but be a little nervous.

"Miss Andrews, it's nice to finally meet you," Miss Standfield greeted Abby with an outstretched hand. She was pretty much what Abby expected. About forty, impeccably dressed in a charcoal-gray business suit with dark hair swept back to the nape of her neck in a severe bun and all business. "Let's dispense with formality. I'm Sylvia, and you are Abby. Is that acceptable?"

"It's fine with me," Abby agreed to the suggestion.

"If you will accompany me, I will show you a little about how we do things around here."

The first stop was a big room full of small cubicles; each one had an easel-like table with a large white paper pad resting on it and different-colored pencils and erasers in racks across the top. That was where the whole process began. It was here that the artists created their original designs.

"How do they know what sort of designs they are supposed to make?" Abby always had a person in mind when she drew up her designs.

"If it's to be a special order, they are informed if it should be formal or informal, long or short, and the approximate size and age of the person who will wear it. If it is to be a stock item, then they are free to use their imagination, and we will determine later how the dress will be finished and where it will go."

The next stop was the pattern room. It was equipped with large tables, each filled with tape measures, pins, chalk, scissors, and an easel at the end of it. Each easel held a chart giving size measurements. At each table, a worker was bent over, intent on the material stretched out on it. They were converting the designs into specific size patterns.

"I notice that some of the tables are using paper and the others are using some sort of fabric to make the patterns. Why is that?" Abby couldn't help but ask.

"If the design is a one of a kind, then we use paper because it will not be used again. If it is to be used more than once, perhaps as a stock item or for a specific line of clothing, then we need to use something a little more substantial," Sylvia explained, pleased that Abby had been so observant. That meant she was interested.

"Since it's approaching noontime, how about a little lunch before we continue?" Sylvia asked as she steered Abby in the direction of the company cafeteria.

After a quick meal, they continued the tour.

The next stop was a room lined with racks and racks of bolts of all sorts of fabrics. Each rack held an array of like colors, displayed from the lightest shade at the top to the deepest shade on the lowest shelf.

Some of the fabrics displayed designs, but the vast majority were solid colors. The room also was equipped with large tables. These tables also held tape measures, pins, chalk, scissors, and patterns; however, bolts of fabric on stands at each table had also been added.

"This is where the fabric is chosen for the design. The choice of fabric can make or break any design. Some designs require a soft flowing fabric, and others need a certain amount of stiffness about them," Sylvia explained the procedure. "In the case of special-order items, the fabric and color usually have been preselected."

Abby remembered the instructor talking about fabric selection and how important it was during her recent training session.

The next area Abby saw was a room full of sewing machines. Workers at every machine were busy with their step in the process. Large carts on wheels were used to transfer the work from machine to machine.

"Why does each worker only do a small part of the sewing?" Abby wondered aloud.

"All the machines look the same, but each one is adapted to only one process. Some sew straight seams. Some are fitted out to make curved seams, like putting in sleeves. Others bind the fabric edges. Some finish the seams, and still others do the hemming. It's faster to pass the work on than change the machine. We have a very high volume of products, so the work has to be streamlined in order to keep up with demand," Sylvia answered.

The next step in the operation they visited was what Sylvia called the trim-and-finish room. The dresses arrived there, hanging on large rolling racks. There were sewing machines there also; each had a torso beside it with a dress on it. These machines were used for making buttonholes and sewing on buttons, snaps, zippers, lace trims, and whatever else the dress needed to put the finishing touches on it.

"We make a lot of special-order, one-of-a-kind items. Therefore, our operation has to be more hands-on than some of the places of mass productions," Sylvia explained. "Well, you've seen most of our operation. We'll skip the warehouses. There's not much to see out there, and it's pretty noisy." Sylvia took Abby back to the cafeteria for a drink and because it was quieter. "Well, what do you think of our operation?" she asked.

"It's amazing! With an operation this big, isn't it difficult to keep track of where everything is at in the process?" Abby wondered.

"We have an excellent support staff. They can tell us where any given piece of product is at any given time." Sylvia assured her they were efficient in every area. "You think about what you've seen today, and come back tomorrow so we can talk again. I have some films to show you a little more about our product lines and where some of our creations go. I think you will be impressed." Sylvia escorted Abby to where her driver was waiting to take her back to the hotel.

"Bring her back here at ten in the morning," Sylvia instructed the driver as he helped Abby into the backseat.

"Yes, ma'am." He tipped his hat in acknowledgment of the order.

"Did you enjoy your day, Miss?" The driver asked, looking at her in his rear-view mirror.

"It is amazing. I didn't realize it was such a big place." Abby had a lot of thinking to do before she could possibly come to any sort of a decision.

"It is pretty good sized. It covers the better part of a square block." The driver filled her in.

Promptly at ten the next morning, Abby walked into Sylvia's waiting room. This time, Sylvia was the one who greeted her.

"Good morning. I hope you slept well. Let's start out down the hall in the film room." Sylvia was all business again today.

Abby spent the next hour and a half viewing films. Sylvia showed her a number of spectacular fashion shows from all over the world in which some of their designs were featured. There was another chronicling the progress of the Fashion House from its inception to present day. The last film was clearly a sales pitch, lauding the benefits of working for the Fashion House.

Afterwards, Sylvia took Abby back to the cafeteria for lunch.

"Well, do you think you could be comfortable joining our family?" Sylvia inquired after they had finished their meal and returned to her office.

"I find your whole operation to be very interesting, and I have been truly impressed with everything I've seen in the last two days. May I have some time to think over what I've seen here before I make a decision?"

"Of course, I know it can't be an easy decision to move halfway across the country by yourself. I'll give you a copy of a contract for you to look over. Plus I've worked up a salary offer and benefits package for you. Take this packet home, and look the papers over. I'll call you in a few days so we can talk again. Your driver will be waiting out front for you. He is at your disposal for the rest of the day. If you want to do a little shopping this afternoon, tell him what you are looking for, and chances are he can suggest the best place to go to find it. Your plane leaves at eleven fifteen tomorrow, I believe. He will be at your hotel at eight-thirty in the morning to take you to the airport. Have a safe trip home." Sylvia escorted Abby to the door of her waiting room. "It's been a distinct pleasure meeting you. We'll be in touch very soon. Good-bye." Sylvia gave Abby a brief handshake and ushered her out the door.

Abby spent the afternoon at her hotel, thinking over what she had seen and heard during her visit at the Fashion House.

On the plane ride home, she made her decision. If she went to work for the Fashion House, she would become just a face in the crowd. She would miss the pleasure of seeing happiness on the face of a client when she tried on a dress that Abby had a hand in creating. She wanted to design dresses for specific people and for specific occasions. She should have known that all along, but it took a talk with her father to get her thinking in the right direction. She was thankful for the opportunity to visit the Fashion House, but that visit was enough to make her realize the things that were the most important in her life.

***

The second Abby arrived home; she was on the phone, calling Witt. The unpacking could wait. This was more important to her. She needed to hear his voice.

"Witt, I just got back and couldn't wait to talk to you." She couldn't believe how happy she was when he answered her call.

"Abby! How did your trip go?" His heart was in his throat. What did she decide? He was afraid to ask, but he had to know.

"It was very nice. I saw a lot of things. That place is quite a big operation. It has worldwide connections," Abby answered.

"I'm glad you got back safely." That wasn't what he wanted to say, but he just couldn't bring himself to ask what he really wanted to know.

"I made up my mind—about the job, I mean." Abby got to the reason for her call.

"What did you decide?" He had to sit down because he was afraid his knees would buckle if he remained standing.

"I have decided this is where I need to be. I was born and raised in Colorado. I am happiest when I'm in Colorado, so why shouldn't I stay where I'm the happiest?" Abby finished. She wanted to tell him she was happiest when she was near him but couldn't form the words.

"Abby, if I were there right now, I would wrap my arms around you and never let you go." Witt dropped his head onto the back of the chair, closed his eyes, and offered a little prayer of thanks.

"I can't wait to see you. Are you coming here this weekend?" Abby asked.

"Try to keep me away!" Witt responded to her question. "If I have to, I will come up by myself, but I think Doug will probably join me."

"I'll let you go and see you this weekend. Come to think of it. That's tomorrow night! It's really good to talk to you, but I want to call Dad." Abby reluctantly disconnected with Witt to call her father.

"Hi, Dad!" she greeted her father when he answered her call.

"It's good to hear your voice. When did you get back?" he asked.

"Just a few minutes ago. I just got through talking to Witt."

"Have you made a decision yet?" He thought he knew what the answer would be, but he wanted her to confirm it.

"They made me an offer, but I'm turning it down. This is where I belong, not in some big city half a country away from my home and family," she answered.

"I'm so glad you came to that realization. This is where we want you too. Come home when you get the chance. Agnes and I would love to see you." Lay was relieved to hear that Abby would be staying put, but all along he had the feeling she wasn't going anywhere.

"How is Agnes? Is she keeping you in line?" Abby inquired.

"She is just fine. I'll tell her you asked about her."

"Give her my love. I'll see you both soon. Good-bye, Dad. I love you." Abby finished the call. It was time to get unpacked and maybe go to Margaret's after she had a bite of lunch. She removed the packet of papers Sylvia had given her. She toyed with the idea of looking at them, but it wouldn't matter what they offered; she knew it would make no difference. She had made the right decision for her, and nothing was going to change her mind.

After she finished putting her clothes away and sat down to eat a sandwich, travel fatigue settled in, so she decided to postpone going to the store until the next day. She sat down to rest a few minutes before thinking about what to fix for dinner. The next thing she knew, Sheryl was shaking her awake.

"I'm sorry. I intended to have dinner ready when you got here. I guess I was more tired than I thought." Abby shook away the last vestiges of sleep as she got up to go to the kitchen.

"Don't keep me in suspense!" Sheryl couldn't wait any longer. "What did you find out while you were gone? Did they make an offer? Have you made a decision yet?"

"They showed me all around their place of business and made me an offer. Every operation there was impressive, but I don't want to be just another face in the crowd. I'm staying put."

"That's great! Does Witt know yet?" Sheryl was ecstatic.

"I called him first thing when I got home. I couldn't wait to talk to him. He's coming in tomorrow evening," Abby answered. "He told me he would be here with or without Doug. He said he wasn't waiting any longer to see me."

"Doug is coming tomorrow evening. We didn't want to invite Witt in case you made the wrong decision. We should have had more faith in you. Your dad told Doug that you weren't going anywhere because you were an Andrews and you would make the right decision. He's the only one who truly believed you would stay here."

"That's my dad!" Abby grinned, really pleased to be an Andrews.

Abby couldn't wait until Witt got there.

Witt insisted on going straight to the apartment instead of checking into the motel first as was their habit. He had waited as long as he could stand it. He had to see her smile and hold her in his arms. The second he saw her, Witt knew he was going to have to take a leap of faith. In that one second, he realized that, no matter how she felt about him, his heart would belong to her forever. He could no longer hold his feelings back.

That weekend was filled with so much happiness and laughter that even a sudden summer rainstorm couldn't dampen their spirits. They wound up ordering lunch in, but no one minded being shut up in the apartment for most of the day. By late afternoon, the rain had passed, and the sun was out, so the group ventured out for dinner and a leisurely stroll in a nearby park before returning to the apartment.

It had been years since any of them had been to Boulder, so they decided to spend the day touring the museums there. Truthfully, they all would have been happy watching grass grow so long as they could have done it together.

All too soon, the weekend was over. Abby's suggestion that the girls go to the ranch for the next weekend was well received. There was always something to do at the ranch, rain or shine.

Sylvia called on Wednesday evening. Abby told Sylvia that she was sorry but she was turning down their offer.

"Is your relocation the main reason you decided against coming on board with us?" Sylvia asked.

"Yes, it's the main reason, but not the only one. My family is here. It's the only place I've ever called home. You have a lot to offer, but it's not for me. I'm sorry I wasted your time and money."

"We really want you and your talent. We are starting a new program, and we would like for you to be a part of it. We haven't worked out all the details yet, but we will help you get set up in an office or perhaps in your home. You will be assigned to special projects—perhaps a line of clothing or one-of-a-kind items for a VIP. It may not be full time at first, so you would still have time to do some private-sector work. For right now, you will be working strictly on spec, but if it works out, you will go on salary," Sylvia explained the offer. "Would you be at all interested in something like that?"

"In other words, I can still do designing for the store here as long as I make time for your special projects and I can remain at home?" Abby asked.

"That's about it. You may have to come here a couple times a year for meetings," Sylvia answered.

"Absolutely! I'm interested. Send me any info you have, and I will look it over."

The next morning, Abby told Margaret about Sylvia's offer.

"Why don't we go to lunch? We need to talk," Carolyn asked.

"It's all right with me," Abby answered, wondering what they needed to talk about this time.

"Could you actually work out of your house if you wanted to?" Carolyn wasted no time in getting to what she wanted to discuss while they waited for their food.

"I guess I can work anywhere I want. She mentioned working out of my house as one possibility," Abby answered.

"I think Carter and I are beginning to get serious about each other, so I'm not in as much of a hurry to leave as I first thought. I know I promised you could have your job back when you were ready, and if you still want it, I'll leave. However, with this new job offer, if you think you might be quitting in the near future, I would like to stay. Working with my mother in this little town isn't nearly as dorky as I thought it would be, especially since I've met Carter McDaniels," Carolyn confessed.

"One of the things Sylvia mentioned was that they might help me get set up in an office. The thought crossed my mind that maybe, at some point, if I could find a vacant building in Everett, I might open up a small store, perhaps patterned after this one. I think Witt and I are beginning to get serious, so it would allow me to be closer to him. Give me a chance to check into that possibility. If it works out and I find a vacant building for a store, we may both get what we want." Abby liked the idea of her own little store in her own hometown.

"Let's don't mention any of this to Mother until we see what can be worked out," Carolyn cautioned.

***

Sheryl loved her new position at the store. Mrs. Jones was scheduled to leave in mid-October, so she was showing Sheryl all she could about buying and stocking merchandise for her department.

Then one day, she had the rug pulled out from under her. News came down from corporate headquarters that they were downsizing their company by closing some of the stores. When the list of closures came out, it included her store. In four months, it would be no more. Some of the long-term employees would be offered transfers if they wished, but most of them would be out of work. Mrs. Jones was notified that her new position at corporate headquarters was still in the planning but delayed until this store closed its doors.

Mrs. Jones offered to give Sheryl a crash course in managing a department, arranging and presenting merchandise. She thought it might help Sheryl to get another job. After four months, Sheryl would be out of a job because she didn't want to transfer anywhere that would take her away from Doug, so she appreciated the help.

Abby called Witt to see if he knew of any vacant building in Everett. She explained what she was thinking of trying to do. He totally approved of the idea and promised that he and Doug would keep their eyes and ears open.

The next time Abby talked to her dad, he asked if Sheryl was having any success at finding a new job, yet.

"I think she's looking but hasn't had much luck. She has until mid-December with the job she has now. She hasn't decided what she wants to do yet. She's keeping an eye on the want ads, but there's just not much out there right now." She felt sorry for Sheryl.

"Doug told me what you are thinking about doing. I think that's a great idea. It's too bad you two girls can't go into business together." Her dad was thinking out loud.

"Yes, that would be great, but I doubt she would want to work in a little store." Abby dismissed the idea.

"It was just a thought," Lay answered. "You're probably right."

"Well, I got to go, Dad. It's time for me to start dinner. I'll call you in a few days. Love you." Abby turned the phone off and set about preparing dinner.

Every day Sheryl pored over the want ads, but without success.

Witt and Doug had so far failed to find a vacant building, but they kept looking every day, determined to find something to get Abby back home. They even considered buying a vacant lot and erecting a building on it but decided that might be a bit too much. She would never accept that kind of help.

Two weeks passed, and Abby still had found nothing nor had Sheryl.

"What are you going to do if you don't find something suitable for your new store?" Carolyn wondered while she and Abby were having lunch one day.

"I can convert the room next to my bedroom into a workroom. Then I will have a place to do whatever the Fashion House gives me. I think I will work on some designs for a portfolio in case I ever need one. Sooner or later, something will open up, and then I will have my store." Abby hastened to assure Carolyn her plans had not changed.

"Don't worry. As long as you will be here to help your mother, I will definitely be leaving."

"I'm beginning to like Carter a lot. I really think I want to stay here where he is, so my plans are becoming more permanent by the day," Carolyn admitted, smiling as she thought about Carter. She was never happier than when she was with him. There was just something about him.

Finally, Witt called Abby with some news. He heard of a business that was closing in about two months. He set up an appointment with the realtor for her on Saturday morning so she could look the property over.

Sheryl jumped at the chance to go to see Doug over the weekend.

Abby asked Witt to go with her when she went to meet the realtor on Saturday. The soon-to-be empty building was located on Main Street next to The Book Store. Its area, with two good-sized rooms and a large storeroom, would serve Abby's needs very well, and it appeared to be in good shape structurally. Witt said he would see to an inspection for her as soon as possible. She tendered a bid on the place, dependent on the outcome of the inspection.

By the time Witt and Abby returned to the ranch, Agnes and Sheryl had a lunch packed for the four of them. Doug had the perfect spot near a small babbling brook for them to have their picnic. They invited Lay and Agnes to go with them, but they both decided they would be much more comfortable sitting in a chair on a screened-in porch than on a blanket on the ground with all the flies and bugs.

By the next weekend, Witt told Abby the inspection had only turned up a couple of minor problems. The owners had agreed to fix them, and they had accepted Abby's offer. She asked Witt to accompany her when she went to meet with all parties involved the next Saturday to start the preliminary paperwork that would make the building hers. It would still be another three weeks before they could finalize the deal.

In the meantime, Sylvia sent Abby a packet containing information about what they were planning for her to do if she accepted their offer. After reading the info, she called Sylvia and agreed to try it. Abby told Sylvia she had found a building to work out of near her home. She also mentioned she was thinking of opening a small dress shop in the front and making the backroom into a workroom for her. Sylvia offered to pay half of the cost of the workroom equipment. Abby readily accepted the offer.

On Monday morning, Abby told Carolyn of the latest developments. They agreed it was time to tell Margaret about the changes coming up. Margaret was happy to hear about Abby's new business venture but was very sorry to lose her. When Carolyn shared her news about her decision to stay in Centerview, Margaret was ecstatic.

She insisted that Abby keep in touch because she had grown very fond of her. Abby promised to do so because she had come to look upon Margaret as a very good friend, and she really wanted to keep up with Carolyn and Carter's romance.

CHAPTER SEVEN

The next weekend, Sheryl accompanied Abby home to see the where the store was to be. They couldn't get in because it was still in use, but at least she could see where it was located and get an idea of the size of the building.

"You know what, Sheryl, Dad mentioned something to me when I first started talking about doing this. He said it was a shame that you and I couldn't make it a joint venture, and I think he's right. I would love it if you could join me as a partner or manager or anything you are comfortable with." Abby broached the subject she had been thinking about since the conversation with her dad.

Sheryl was surprised at the offer. Then she answered thoughtfully, "I am learning a lot about managing a business. Between what I picked up at the training session we attended and what Mrs. Jones is showing me, I don't think I would have any problem running the store while you do the designing. Mother taught me some basic sewing, so I might even be able to do some of the simple sewing to help you at first, but when we get a little busier, we may have to hire a professional." Sheryl paused and then laughed self-consciously. "Listen to me. I'm already telling you what we need, and we don't even have the store yet. If you are sure you want a partner, you have one." Sheryl didn't have to think very long to make her decision. Going into business with her best friend seemed like the natural thing to do.

"Oh, Sheryl! It'll be a dream come true! Wait until the guys hear about this!" Abby was excited that Sheryl and she were going to be in business together.

"They're really going to be surprised when we tell them we are going to be partners in the dress shop!" Sheryl completely missed the obvious.

"Well, that too. What I was talking about was that, at some point, we will both be moving back to Everett," Abby explained.

"Oh, my gosh! I didn't even think about that! That's even better. How soon can we tell them?" Sheryl was really excited now.

"If you are absolutely certain you want to take a chance with me, I don't see why we can't tell them this evening." Abby didn't want to wait any longer to tell Witt.

Witt and Doug were in the living room when the girls found them.

"Sheryl, what do you think about the location of Abby's store?" Doug asked as soon as they walked in the door.

"It's a great location. The bookstore next door is bound to generate some foot traffic. It's in a highly visible spot, right on Main Street." Sheryl was already thinking about the success of the new store. "Plus, there's not another store like it in town."

"We do have some other news though." Abby paused for effect.

"What?" Witt asked.

"We are going to be partners in the store!" Sheryl added, looking at Abby while they waited to see if the guys would pick up the rest of their news.

"Hey! That's great. It's sure to be a success if you two join forces." Doug was happy for them.

Witt started to join in when suddenly he stopped dead still. "Hey! If you both are going to work in the new store, doesn't that mean you both will be moving back here?" he asked.

"We think we will have to," Abby answered, laughing at them. For a second, the guys looked at each other, then let out bloodcurdling war whoops, grabbed the girls in bear hugs, and started swinging them around.

"What's all the ruckus?" Lay and Agnes heard the noise from the front porch and came in to see what was going on.

"Abby and Sheryl are going to be partners in the new store, and they are moving back home!" Doug filled them in.

"Hallelujah! That's the best news I've had since Agnes agreed to marry me." Lay grabbed Agnes and waltzed her around the room. "This calls for a celebration! Dinner's on me at Duggin's." Lay wanted to celebrate getting his family back together again.

All too soon, Sunday evening came, and it was time for the girls to return to their apartment.

Sheryl was going tell Mrs. Jones about her new enterprise with Abby. She intended to ask if Mrs. Jones would be willing to teach her some things she would need to know when she took over stocking and managing the new store.

Abby brought Margaret and Carolyn up to date about the partnership and the store.

"Do you have any idea when you will be making the move to Everett?" Carolyn asked Abby sometime later that day.

"Not yet. We don't take possession for another three weeks. I guess it will be along about then." She hadn't given any thought as to when the move would take place.

"If I'm going to stay here, I need to get my own place. Mother's been great, but I'm sure she will be happy to get her privacy back." Carolyn continued, "I was wondering if I would be able to rent your apartment when you leave."

"I'll ask Sheryl. She has the lease, but I don't remember when it's out," Abby answered. "It might be that you could sublet and take over her lease."

"That would be great. Let me know, please." That suited Carolyn fine.

***

Mrs. Jones was more than happy to give Sheryl a crash course in the starting up and the stocking of a new store. Margaret offered to help the girls locate display stands, cabinets, and tables for their merchandise.

Abby had to make a trip back to the Fashion House to sign some contracts. This time, no one minded her going. While she was there, Sylvia helped her locate some of the equipment she would need. She then made arrangements to purchase what she would need for her workroom and have it delivered at the appropriate time. Sylvia advised her which of the companies had the best books of fabric swatches and which ones carried the best selections of materials.

Sheryl was busy making lists of supplies they would need to open the store. Mrs. Jones made suggestions as to what should be on those lists and advised her where to find the best places to get them. Abby made her list of the supplies she would need for her workroom plus the basic fabrics she would need to stock her shelves with and got everything ordered.

The time had come to make the move back to Everett. Witt, Doug, and Lay helped them accomplish it in a couple of days. Carolyn made arrangements to sublet their apartment, so the men helped her get moved in as soon as Abby and Sheryl vacated the space.

Soon, all the tables, counters, and clothing racks were in place, and it was time to start stocking their store. They had decided to pattern it after Margaret's business. They stocked a few modestly priced but well-made dresses and a variety of other feminine garments. Abby's equipment was delivered on time. Witt and Doug helped her get it set up. Soon everything was stocked, and they were ready to have a grand opening.

The only thing missing was a name for the business. Lay suggested it be called By Design. No one had a better idea, so Doug painted a sign to put up over the doorway.

That first day, there were a number of curiosity lookers, but Sheryl thought of that as a good thing. She figured the more people who came into the store and looked over their merchandise, the better the chances were that they would pass the word along about what kind of garments the store carried. In turn, they were more likely to have people coming in to purchase something.

Business was brisk for the little store. On the third day, Abby had her first client. It was Katherine Tracy.

"Hello, Abby. I'm sorry I didn't make it into town for your grand opening," she apologized to Abby. "It's always good to see a new business open here in Everett."

"We are happy to be here. It's nice to see you again, Katherine." She accepted the apology. "How have you been?"

"I'm really getting along very well," she answered.

"Katherine, I would like you to meet my partner, Sheryl Barry," Abby introduced Sheryl.

"Hello, Sheryl. I think I've seen you around. Aren't you Agnes Barry's daughter?"

"Yes. I think we've met, but it has been a while. I've been living in Centerview since I got out of college," Sheryl explained.

"It's great that both of you girls have come back home. I hope your store does well." Katherine wished them success.

"How may we help you, Mrs. Tracy?" Sheryl asked.

"Actually, I'm here to see Abby." Katherine turned to Abby.

"What can I do for you?" Abby asked.

"It happens that I need a dress for a very special occasion, and I was hoping you might have time to make it for me." Katherine explained why she was there.

"I will be happy to create a special dress for you. Do you mind if I ask what the occasion is?" Abby couldn't think of anything going on locally.

"Actually, my son is getting married," Katherine explained.

"Tyler is getting married?" Abby was shocked.

"Yes, Jennifer is a wonderful girl. After all he put her through, she still loves him. We found an excellent psychologist who took Tyler on as a patient. I can tell a big difference in him already. He still has a long way to go, but he is so much better than he was four months ago. Gerald and I have gone to a few sessions to try to understand a little more about what we can do to help Tyler." Katherine brought Abby up to date.

"I am so thankful you found the right help for him. Maybe he can be happy now." Abby was glad for Katherine and for Tyler.

"When I told him I was coming here today, he wanted me to ask you if he could come and talk with you sometime. I think he wants to apologize to you again." Katherine hesitated to ask Abby to see him again.

"Yes. Tell him to come by the store sometime. I would be glad to talk to him again." She guessed it wouldn't hurt to hear what he had to say as long as they weren't alone. She still had a few doubts about his 'recovery'.

A customer entered the store, so Sheryl went to help her, and Abby showed Katherine to her workroom in the back.

"Katherine, if you will stand here, I will get your measurements. Then we will talk about the dress." Abby began the process of making her first dress in her new shop. "Tell me, what sort of dress do you have in mind?" she asked.

"Well, it will be a spring wedding—in early May. Perhaps something with a removable jacket. Then if it's warm, I can slip out of it. Maybe an A-line skirt, well below my knees." Katherine explained what she was thinking about.

"That's enough to get me started. If you will give me a few minutes, I can draw up a couple of designs for you to look at." Abby already had some things in mind.

"How about I come back in two or three days? That way, you won't be rushed," Katherine suggested.

"That would be fine." That would give her time to think about the designs. This was going to have to be a very special dress. Of course, for Abby, they were all very special.

By the time Katherine returned, Abby had three designs ready for her to look at.

"I don't know. I like all of them. I can't decide. Which one do you like best, Abby?" She couldn't make up her mind.

"Well, let's look at fabrics. Often, what you choose will lead you to the style the dress should be. Sometimes, the way the fabric drapes makes all the difference." Abby would rather the client choose the design because oftentimes, they were more comfortable with the finished product if they made the choice themselves.

After several tentative choices, Katherine finally settled on a taffeta fabric. Jennifer had chosen pastel colors for the wedding, so she decided on a soft peach which complimented her coloring and dark hair.

Abby showed Katherine the three drawings again. This time, Katherine immediately was drawn to one of them. It was the same one Abby would have chosen.

"I've never had a dress made before, so what happens now?" Katherine asked Abby.

"First, I order the fabric you have chosen. While I'm waiting for that, I'll transfer your measurements onto paper to make the pattern that I will use to make your dress. When the fabric comes in, I transfer that pattern to your fabric, cut the pieces out, and assemble them together. When I get all the pieces joined together and the dress begins to take shape, then I will call you to come in for a fitting. That's when I begin to adjust the fit exactly to you. I'll have you come in for another fitting when I get it put together except for the trim. Next you will come in for a final fitting. Generally, there are still a few minor alterations with that fitting to adjust the fit exactly the way you feel comfortable with. Then the dress is finished."

"That's sounds complicated." Katherine shook her head.

"It's not that difficult. I really love doing this kind of work, so that makes it easy." Abby laughed at her expression.

"If you say so." Katherine shook her head and laughed. "Before I go, Tyler wanted me to ask if he could come to see you later this morning."

"It would be fine with me." Abby was going to ask Sheryl to be sure to stay in the store while he was there. She couldn't help but have some doubts about Tyler.

Tyler entered the store an hour and a half later.

"Hello, Abby. Do you have a few minutes to talk?" he quietly asked her.

"Good morning, Tyler. Won't you come in?" Abby was standing in the doorway of her workroom. She stepped back so he could go into the backroom. She made sure the door was left wide open.

"I wanted to come and apologize again for the way I treated you. Did Mother tell you I've started in therapy?" he asked Abby.

"Yes, she told me," she answered, waiting to hear what else he had to say.

"I've told you so many lies in the past that I just had to come here to straighten things out and apologize to you in person again." Tyler sounded sincere, but still she waited. "When I told you our mothers had been sorority sisters, I was not telling you the truth. They didn't even know each other. They weren't forcing us to get married either. Jennifer and I were introduced at a party given by a mutual friend. I fell hard for her the first time I saw her. Before long, I found myself proposing to her—much too soon. When I thought about what I had done, I got scared. I was afraid of being tied down for the rest of my life to someone I didn't really know. My doctor has helped me see that. I told you all those lies to get you to go out with me. If Jennifer had found out about us, subconsciously I hoped she would break the engagement. I was desperate to have a fling with somebody, in the hopes that someone would tell Jennifer. I chose you because you were there. But then, when she did find out about us and actually broke the engagement, I realized I really did love her and couldn't bear to lose her. She told me the only way she would come back to me was if I went into therapy. I was desperate. I would have done anything to get her back." Tyler tried to explain his actions. "I'm learning a lot about myself and why I acted the way I did. I know I have a long way to go, but now that I can understand a lot about my actions in the past, I realize how abominably I have treated you. I hope that someday you can forgive me for how badly I acted toward you." Tyler hoped she would understand.

"I'm glad you are getting the help you need, Tyler. In a way, I think I do understand why you acted the way you did, and I do accept your apology. I hope you continue with your therapy because it seems to be helping." Abby accepted Tyler's apology, with some reservations. She couldn't help but wonder how sincere he really was. She hoped he was serious with his words, saying them not only because he felt it was something he needed to do, but also because he truly meant what he was saying.

"Well, I'd better go. I need to get Mother's car back to her. Mine is in the shop, so she let me use hers this morning." Tyler prepared to leave.

"Congratulations on your upcoming marriage. I hope you will be very happy." Abby walked him to the door.

"Thank you. Good-bye, ladies." Tyler bid them farewell as he left.

"He sounded sincere enough," Sheryl commented.

"I hope he is really serious in getting help, not just putting on a front." Abby couldn't help but still have her doubts. She guessed time would tell.

***

One evening, Lay and Agnes announced that they planned to get married on February 14th. They also had come to a couple of other decisions.

"We don't need this big old house, so as soon as the weather breaks next spring, we are going to build a smaller house down the road apiece." Lay explained the first part.

"I know I should have talked with you both before I came to this next decision, but since you'll be getting a new house when you get married, Abby, I would like for Doug to stay here in this house." Lay waited for their reaction.

"Are you sure you want to do that, Dad?" Doug asked after a moment. "It doesn't feel right for you to leave and me to stay."

"Dad, this is your home. Are you sure you want to leave it?" Abby thoughts reflected Doug's. She hadn't mentioned it to anyone, but she was beginning to believe Witt had given up on marrying her. Things had been different ever since a few days after they had opened the store. At first, things seemed normal, and he was with her as often as they had time. Then things changed. He seemed to have backed off their relationship. He stopped coming around at all. So it might be a while before she got married, if ever.

"Agnes and I have talked about this at great length, and we agree we don't need all this room. After we're married, we would like to do a little traveling, so a smaller house will suit us just fine. We found a certain spot on a little hill south of here that has a beautiful view, and there are trees already there for shade. It would be the perfect location for our new home." Lay looked to Agnes for agreement.

"It would be a beautiful spot to retire to," Agnes added.

"Well, Dad, if you are sure this is what you want. I certainly have no objection." Abby approved of her dad's decision. "The house is yours, Doug."

"And it's your home for as long as you wish, Abby," Doug reluctantly agreed.

"There, that's settled. Now let's go out and eat at Duggin's to seal the deal." Lay invited everyone to go. "Abby, why don't you call Witt to see if he can go with us?"

"I think he was going to be doing something this evening. I don't remember what." She really didn't want to call him.

"I talked to him this afternoon. He didn't say anything about being busy tonight. Let me call him," Doug offered. He knew there was something going on with Witt and Abby, but he hadn't yet figured out exactly what it was.

When Witt told Doug he didn't feel up to going out to dinner, he knew there definitely had to be a problem. Witt never turned down a chance to be with Abby. Doug was going to have to talk to both of them to see if he could get to the bottom of it. Probably he should talk to Sheryl first to see if Abby had mentioned anything to her. It had to be some kind of a misunderstanding. They were too perfect for each other to not be together.

Abby tried to put up a good front at dinner, but Doug knew her well enough to know it was forced. She was glad when the evening was over and she was in her room. She felt like she was losing her best friend and didn't know what to do about it.

She was glad when the weekend was over and she could go back to her store. Work gave her something else to think about.

Agnes went to the store that afternoon with a twofold reason for being there.

"I wanted to ask if you would possibly have time to make a dress for me to be married in," she asked Abby.

"Agnes, I would be honored to make your dress." Abby had been expecting that and knew despite how she felt, she had to make

150

a very special one for her. "If you will come with me, we'll get started on it." She led Agnes to the backroom so she could take her measurements. "Tell me a little about what kind of dress you want." Abby asked while she took down the information she needed.

"I haven't given it much thought. Perhaps something with lace, fairly simple, maybe with a small hat. And I suppose I'll need shoes to match."

"Do you have a color in mind?"

"I don't know. Maybe lavender or mauve," Agnes answered.

"Let's look at some fabric samples. Maybe you will see something that you like," Abby suggested.

After much deliberation, Agnes settled on a soft orchid silk fabric. "Do you think that shade would look all right on me?"

"I think that is a beautiful color for you," Abby assured her. "If you will come back in a couple of days, I will have some designs for you to look at."

Abby would need some time to design the perfect dress for Agnes.

"That isn't the only reason I came here today." Agnes hesitated to bring up the subject. "I hope you don't think I am meddling, but I have noticed you don't seem happy anymore. Is there anything I can do to make you feel better? I'm guessing it has to do with your reluctance to call Witt the other evening and his turning down the dinner invitation with us."

"You picked up on that, did you? I was hoping no one had noticed." She thought she had fooled them all. "Do the others know?" she asked.

"I haven't said a word to anyone," Agnes promised.

"Truthfully, I really don't understand what's going on right now, so I don't know what can be done to help. I would just as soon everyone stayed out of it until I have time to try to sort things out myself." Abby preferred to keep things to herself until she had time to try to come to terms with the situation with Witt. "Please don't mention what you think to anyone else, even Sheryl," Abby pleaded.

"I won't tell a soul, but you know your father. He is good at picking up on things. Sooner or later, he is going to notice if Witt stops coming around as often as usual." Agnes understood Lay well enough to know it was only a matter of time.

"I'll cross that bridge when he figures it out. Maybe by then, I'll have things sorted out for myself." Abby sighed. She sure hoped so anyway.

"I'll be back in two or three days. In the meantime, if there is anything I can do, please just ask." Agnes wished she could console the girl but didn't know what to do. She stopped to visit with Sheryl for a moment on her way out.

"Take care of our girl," she reminded Sheryl in a low voice so Abby wouldn't hear.

"I'm trying, but she won't let me do much," Sheryl replied.

Doug spent some time thinking about a plan of action to get Witt and Abby back together. He needed to start by talking to Sheryl. Maybe she would have some more thoughts on the subject.

"Has Abby mentioned anything about what's happening between Witt and her?" Doug asked Sheryl the first time he got her alone.

"No. She just stopped talking about him. I've tried asking her about it, but she just says she can't discuss it yet. Something happened, but I don't have any idea as to what it is. The thing is, I'm not sure she knows what happened. Witt just quit coming around."

Sheryl was worried about Abby. The girl was losing weight and never laughed anymore. The circles under her eyes were a clear indication she wasn't sleeping well.

"We've got to do something! Have you talked to Witt?" Sheryl asked.

"Not yet. I don't know if he will even talk to me about what's going on." Doug was at a loss, but he knew he couldn't let it alone.

"Well, you won't know until you try. It's up to us to do something to get them to talk again." Sheryl would try anything to help her friend.

"I'll go see him. Maybe if I ask him straight out what's going on with them, he'll tell me about it. He can't do any more than tell me to mind my own business." Doug decided he didn't have a choice; he had to try to do something.

Doug spent the rest of the afternoon trying to figure out what he was going to say to Witt.

Sheryl waited for an opportunity to talk to Abby again. They were pretty busy at the store, so if Sheryl was free, then Abby was with someone. That was good for business, but it gave them little time to talk.

Katherine came in for her last fitting. She was very pleased with the way the dress looked and felt on her.

"I think you should be able to pick it up next week. It won't take me long to make these few small adjustments." Abby was satisfied with the way the dress turned out also.

"When he was here, did Tyler tell you that he and Jennifer have decided to stay in Everett?"

"No, he didn't mention it." Abby was surprised.

"He decided he wants to stay here and learn more about running the ranch, and Jennifer agreed to move here. He's actually been going out with his father to learn how to do some of the work. Gerald and I are giving them a piece of land, and we're going to have a house built on it for them. They are both looking over floor plans now. It will be so nice to have them living nearby," Katherine explained.

After several people came in to ask if Abby would do alterations, they decided it might be in their best interest to add tailoring as part of their service. That turned out to be a wise move on their part. Most days, Abby had all the work that she could handle. She was thankful to be kept busy because she had less time to think when her hands were busy.

Doug got his chance to talk to Witt one day when he called to ask if Doug would come over to help him install a new gate.

After the work was done, they cooled off on the front porch with some lemonade.

"I've missed you coming around. Is there something going on between you and Abby?" He opened the conversation.

"No, there's absolutely nothing going on between us. I don't want talk about it. Maybe sometime down the road, we will discuss it, but right now, it's too soon." Witt emptied his glass and got up.

"I've got things to do. I'll see you later. Thanks for your help with putting up the gate."

"When you want to talk, I'll be here. If there is anything I can do to help, just tell me. You two need to be together. You're perfect for each other," Doug offered.

"I know that, but apparently she doesn't," Witt answered as he walked off the porch, leaving Doug at a complete loss as to what that cryptic answer could possibly mean. It didn't make any sense.

He could only hope Sheryl would have more luck with her talk with Abby.

Finally, one evening just before closing time, Sheryl got her chance. The girls were relaxing a few minutes before heading home.

"Abby, I hate to bring this up again, but isn't there anything I can do to help you get through this? I know you are hurting. You're losing weight, you're not sleeping at night, and you never laugh. You can't go on like this." She stopped for a moment and looked around the store. "You're living your dream, but you're not enjoying it, and that's not fair. It shouldn't be this way because you deserve to be happy. Won't you please tell me what's happened between you and Witt?"

"Thanks for being concerned about me. If you could help, I'd let you, but this something I have to figure out for myself." Abby slowly got out of her chair and, with a deep sigh, added, "It's time to close up and go home."

Abby had been going over and over in her mind her last conversations with Witt. She didn't have any idea what had happened. The last time they were together had certainly been friendly. He had embraced her and kissed her good-bye and told her he would see her later.

That was the last time he had spoken to her or come by the store. If only she knew what had happened. She should just ask him, but her pride wouldn't let her do that. She understood Witt still went over to see Doug, but only when she wasn't there. He was avoiding her, and she didn't understand why. What could she have done to cause him to be so angry with her? She forced herself to eat something and take part in the conversation at the dinner table every evening, but all she really wanted to do was stay up in her room, curled up in a chair by herself.

She was certain her dad suspected something was wrong by now, but so far, he had refrained from asking her about it. Part of her wanted to talk to him and maybe get his advice, but what good would that do? He couldn't help any more than the others. It was her problem to try to understand.

***

The little store was thriving. Tailoring had become a large part of their business. The Fashion House regularly sent projects for Abby to do. Frequently, they asked for a one-of-a-kind style for the wife of an important person. Sometimes it was a series of designs using the same fabric, or once in a while, they just wanted suggestions for fabrics to be used for previously drawn product lines. Abby quite often needed to work late in order to meet some of the deadlines. She was happy to do that because it was a distraction for her. She was about to drive herself crazy, going over and over in her mind her last meeting with Witt. Why couldn't she just move on? Obviously, their romance, or whatever it was, had ended. Witt was through with her. Why couldn't she just stop dreaming about him at night?

At times, Abby felt like time was standing still, but before she knew it, Thanksgiving was upon them.

Lay asked Hank and Elizabeth to come over for Thanksgiving Day dinner. They said they would let him know after they talked to Witt.

Elizabeth called Agnes the next day. She explained that they wouldn't be there because Witt wanted to stay home and they didn't want to leave him home alone on Thanksgiving Day.

"Agnes, do you have any idea what is going on with Witt and Abby?" Elizabeth asked.

"I wish I knew." Agnes sighed. "Abby won't talk about it."

"Witt won't talk to us either. He's working from daylight till dark and spends a lot of time sitting on the porch alone. If one of us joins him, he thinks of something he has to do and leaves. I don't think he's sleeping much because I hear him pacing around in his room all hours of the night. It's breaking my heart because I don't know what to do to make him feel better." Elizabeth was worried about Witt.

"I'm sorry you can't come over Thursday, but I understand. Abby isn't my daughter, but I feel like she is, and you hurt when your child hurts, but you don't know what to do about it. I guess all we can do is continue to try. Maybe one of them will eventually tell us what's going on. I'll talk to you in a day or two," Agnes concluded their conversation, just as frustrated as Elizabeth was.

A blizzard moved in on the day before Thanksgiving. Abby and Sheryl decided to close the store at noon before they got snowed in. The roads sometimes were impassible for days, and they didn't want to be stranded at their store. After driving around and through rapidly growing snowdrifts, they finally pulled into the driveway. Doug had shoveled a space for their car and a path for them to walk to the house.

"We're so glad you're finally home." Agnes met them at the door. "We were worried about you on the road in this weather."

"There's no place like home, especially when there's a blizzard outside." Sheryl was thankful to be there also.

They had decided earlier to close the store until Monday. As it turned out, it was just as well. The blizzard continued for the rest of that day and all through Thanksgiving Day. Doug and some of the ranch hands spent a big part of the day checking to be sure the livestock had access to wind breaks for shelter, food to eat, and the heated stock tanks were working so they had water to drink. Dinner was put off until later in the day because the animals had to be tended to before the men would take time to eat their meal.

By five, everyone had finished the outside work. The ranch hands had been invited to join the family for dinner. As soon as they all got warmed up, dinner was served.

It was tradition in the family to have everyone hold hands around the table and say what they were thankful for. One by one each took their turn, all the while wondering what Abby was going to say when it became her turn.

"I am thankful for my family and my work." She had spent a lot of time thinking what she was going to say. She wished it could be different, but it wasn't, so she had to accept it.

***

The sun came up to a clear blue sky the next morning. The landscape was covered with pristine snow that glistened in the sunlight like diamonds, with snowdrifts taller than the men and icicles hanging off every structure. At first glimpse, it took your breath away. It was a perfect winter wonderland with graceful swirls of snow more beautiful than any artist would ever be able to portray. Mother Nature had outdone herself.

After breakfast, the work began for the men. The cattle and horses had to be tended to, and then paths had to be carved out of the snow for passages to the outbuildings. A tractor equipped with a blade cleaned off the driveway and parts of the walkways, but the rest had to be done by hand.

By evening, the immediate work was done. The ranch hands returned to the bunkhouse after dinner with invitation to have all their meals with the family. Normally, they would have gone home to their families, but that wasn't possible because they were stranded like everyone else.

Doug and Sheryl were enjoying their time together. There was a good supply of board games and puzzles in a closet. They decided to assemble a jigsaw puzzle of the US Capitol building. Happy as they were, it was impossible to get Abby out of their minds. Sheryl went up to Abby's bedroom to ask her to join them.

"We're going to put a jigsaw puzzle together in the living room. Why don't you come down and help us? It would be more fun than sitting up here by yourself." Sheryl stuck her head in the door to talk to Abby.

"Maybe later." She was sitting curled up in a chair, staring out the window. "The snow is so beautiful across the fields with the sun shining on it. It's kind of soothing just to look at it." She turned her head to smile sadly at her friend.

"Come down when you feel like it. We would love to have a couple of extra hands." Sheryl withdrew and returned downstairs.

Doug had the puzzle spread out on the card table when she returned. From the number of pieces on the table, it looked like it was going to be a weekend-long project.

Lay and Agnes were in the dining room with house plans spread out on the table. They were trying to pick the floor plan they liked best for their new house. When they got tired of looking at house plans, they brought out the travel brochures from faraway places, trying to decide where they would spend their honeymoon. It definitely had to be somewhere warm.

Agnes prepared a pot of chili for dinner. That—along with potato salad, coleslaw, and deviled eggs—left from the day before served very well for the evening meal.

Doug called Abby down for dinner. She managed to eat a little, and as soon as the meal was eaten and the kitchen cleaned, she disappeared back to her room.

Lay had let Abby alone without comment so far, but it was time for her come downstairs, not sit in her room. With that in mind, he went up to have a talk with her.

"May I come in?" he asked as he knocked on her door.

"Of course, you're always welcome." She could count on one hand the number of times her father had been to her bedroom.

He stood for a moment, looking at her dejected body curled up in the chair by the window, before he took a chair near hers.

"Oh, Abby." He sighed deeply before beginning. "I can't help but see that you are hurting. I would give anything if I could take that pain away, but the fact is, I can't. I'm not going to ask you what's wrong. In the end, it's really not important because pain is pain no matter the source. It's not going to go away as long as you sit up here by yourself. That's not how you deal with it. There are four other people in this house that are worried about you and want to help, but as long as you sit up here, they can't. It's time for you to come back downstairs and rejoin the family. You will be surprised at how much better you'll feel if you help put that jigsaw puzzle together. Actually,

I think they need your help. You always could work circles around Doug when it came to most puzzles or games."

"Could I have this one last night here by myself?" Abby asked after a moment.

"As long as it's your last, I guess I'll give you that." Lay stood, leaned down to give his daughter a tender kiss on the forehead, quietly left the bedroom, and returned to the living room to sit on the couch with Agnes.

"Mission accomplished. I think she'll be down in the morning," Lay quietly told Agnes.

"Did she tell you what's wrong?" Agnes asked.

"I didn't ask. That might be part of the problem. Too many questions are being asked of her. If she's not ready to talk about what's bothering her, then perhaps we need to respect her wishes and leave her alone. They'll figure it out. If she and Witt are meant to be together, then they will be. It's out of our hands."

The whole family ate breakfast together the next morning. Abby helped clean the kitchen afterwards and offered to cut up some vegetables for the soup Agnes was preparing for their evening meal, then joined Doug and Sheryl to work on the jigsaw puzzle.

"How long have you two been working on this puzzle?" she asked when she sat down and surveyed the table.

"We started on it late yesterday afternoon and worked most of last evening," Sheryl answered.

"And this is all you have done? At this rate, it will be the spring thaw before you will be able to see the capitol building on this table. It's a good thing I'm here. You need help." Abby picked up a piece of the puzzle and immediately laid it into its proper place.

Doug and Sheryl looked at each other with raised eyebrows. It was good to see a little of the old Abby. Maybe she was back.

By evening, the puzzle was completed. They debated starting another one but decided on a game of monopoly instead. They set up the board and played for a couple of hours before they called it a night.

"Thank you, Dad. You were right." Abby kissed her father before she went upstairs.

"Of course, I'm always right!" he answered, tongue in cheek.

"I wouldn't say that. But on this case, I'll give you one." Abby gave him a second peck on the cheek before going up to bed.

She slept better that night than she had for some time. She woke up hungry; she hadn't had an appetite for a while either. Maybe she was over the worst of it. She was actually looking forward to the day.

Lay learned their road wasn't scheduled to be plowed until Monday afternoon, so everyone was given an extra day at home. That meant the Monopoly game was on again after they attended to the stock. After a couple of hours, it was becoming very evident as to who was going to be the winner. Abby took no prisoners. She quickly took over ownership of most of the hotels and railroads. Rental fees were rapidly depleting any money Doug and Sheryl managed to accumulate. Clearly, luck and skill was on Abby's side. By noon, Doug was broke, and Sheryl had very little cash left, so she threw in the towel, thus conceding the victory to Abby.

"What do you want to play now?" Abby was on a roll, so she wanted another game.

"It's not going to be another game, I can promise you that. Coming in last to two women has almost wrecked my ego. It's taken just about as much as it can stand for now. I'm going to see if I can find a movie to watch. I'm going to try to pop some corn. Does anyone else want anything?" Doug vetoed any more games.

"Yeah. While you are up, bring me some iced tea, please." Sheryl took him up on the offer.

"I'd like the same, please. Put my tea in a tall glass with plenty of ice and a straw. I would also like a bowl of popcorn with lots of butter." Abby put her request in, grinning as he turned around, looked at her, and frowned. It was good to have her back. But he was still going to try to find out what happened between her and Witt.

As for Abby, she was just happy to feel like teasing her brother again. She silently thanked her dad again for that.

***

Tuesday morning found Sheryl and Abby back in the store and with a full slate of work.

"I think you are going to need some help pretty soon." Sheryl looked at all the orders Abby had waiting for her. "This tailoring part of the business is where you are behind."

"It might not hurt. I've been working longer hours than I really want to," Abby agreed. "Why don't we advertise in the local *Gazette* and the *Weekly Shopper?* Maybe we could find someone locally. If people know her, it might be good for business."

Sheryl was already thinking how to word the ad. She probably should have Abby do the interviewing because she would know what she was looking for. Besides she would be the one who would be working closely with anyone who came on board.

Within a week, Abby had found her helper, Sarah Porter, a lady whose family was grown and gone from home. She had worked for herself for some time but grew tired of the headaches of it and wanted to work for someone else. She was well known for her alterations and expected that some of her clients would follow her.

Sarah proved to be an excellent seamstress and a very nice person. Sheryl and Abby immediately liked her. She took over the alteration side of the business, leaving Abby free to do her designing.

The Fashion House was demanding more of Abby's time. They had come to see Abby as very good at anything they asked of her. They used her mostly for what they considered the more important of their assignments. Most often, they wanted one-of-a-kind dresses for VIP wives around the world. Abby didn't know it yet, but her name was growing in popularity as she became known for her unique creations.

One day Abby happened to notice Witt's pickup drive past their store. A wave of deep indescribable sorrow invaded her body. If she only knew why Witt disliked her so, maybe she could accept the situation and move on with her life.

Sheryl also noticed him. She could almost hate Witt for the way he treated her friend. Doug was still trying to find out what happened, but Witt refused to explain. Whenever Doug tried to broach the subject, Witt just said 'not yet' and walked away.

The only clue Doug had came from the first time he asked Witt about it. When he told Witt that they were perfect for each other, Witt had replied, 'I know that, but apparently she doesn't.' What could he have meant by that? He and Sheryl had discussed it to no avail. Apparently, Witt thought Abby had done something to betray him. But what could it be?

***

Christmas was rapidly approaching. Abby threw herself into decorating the house and store.

The three of them decorated a small tree for the store, and Abby strung garland and strings of lights all around the store, inside and out. Every night she had something new to hang somewhere at home. Their tree at home was all of seven feet tall. They all spent one Saturday filling the branches with the trinkets she had brought home. Doug teased her that they wouldn't be able to tell the tree was green if they used all the stuff she brought home. She threatened to go out and chop down second tree to decorate if he didn't use them on the one they had. She had plans for every room to be decorated, including the bedrooms. Lay and Doug banned her from their rooms as did Sheryl, so she gave up on the bedroom idea and concentrated to all the living spaces.

The pile of brightly wrapped gifts grew under the tree. By Christmas Eve, it had spread out all around the tree. It was a happy time for all. Abby did her best to put on a happy face, but everyone knew it was an act. No one mentioned it, so she thought she had pulled it off. The time she dreaded most was New Year's Eve. She overheard Doug and Sheryl making plans for that night, and she was sure her dad and Agnes would have something planned. No matter what they did, if she joined them, she would be a third wheel.

Lay knew the quandary Abby must be in, so he made a suggestion that they have a New Year's Eve party. Agnes agreed and began taking stock of the food they had on hand and making a list for what they would need, while Lay invited the people to attend his party. He was sure there had to be some who had no plans. Though he didn't expect them to attend, he called Hank and Elizabeth. They were sorry, but they would be unable to be there.

In short order, they had twenty-five guests coming. He stipulated it was to be a casual party. The reason behind that was because he didn't want to have to dress up.

Agnes planned a buffet. It required less preparation and would be easier to serve. She gave the girls a list of things she needed, and they promised to bring the items home that evening.

Abby liked the idea of a party. She would have to thank her dad later. She probably would not be the only single person there, so maybe she could enjoy herself.

By the time people began to arrive, the tables for cards, jigsaw puzzles, and various board games for all ages were set up in the den, one corner of the living room had been cleared for dancing, and the music discs were placed by the stereo for music. A fire was burning in the fireplace for those who preferred to just sit and talk. The buffet table was loaded with all kinds of foods and drinks. Tables were set up for those who wanted to sit down to eat.

Agnes, Sheryl, and Abby kept a close eye on the food to be sure there was plenty for everyone.

When all was said and done, one could say a good time was had by all, even Abby. Three of their guests were girls Abby had gone to school with. They spent the evening catching up on the happenings since the last time they had seen one another. They were duly impressed by Abby's career. They had heard about By Design but didn't know Abby and Sheryl were the proprietors.

The new year dawned clear and cold with the promise of more snow coming in. The weathermen were expecting it to be another blizzard.

The men spent the day getting extra feed out for the livestock and double-checking on the water tanks. They made sure all of the animals had access to either a shed or a windbreak so they could get out of the raw wind. By early evening, the wind had picked up, and the snow was beginning to fall.

By dark, the storm had become a full-blown blizzard with gale-force winds and heavy snow. The next morning, there was another winter wonderland much like the Thanksgiving Day storm. The snow was still falling heavily, so it would do no good to work on the walkways. As soon as they tended the livestock, everyone returned to the house to pass away the time while they waited for the snow to stop.

Sheryl wanted to play another game of Monopoly, but Doug vetoed that. His ego didn't want to take another beating, and he knew it would if Abby was involved. He never could beat that girl! Instead, he suggested another jigsaw puzzle because he knew there would be no winners or losers there.

Lay joined them for a little while and then went off in search of Agnes. By late afternoon, the storm had subsided. After checking on the livestock, the men worked on the walks until darkness overtook them. After a late evening meal, everyone retired early because they would have a lot of snow to move the next day.

By the end of the next day, the roads were open, so it was time to return to work.

***

Abby asked Agnes to come into the store for another fitting. The dress was nearing completion, so one more fitting, and it should be ready.

Sheryl and Abby were helping Agnes with the final wedding plans. She and Lay wished to have the wedding at the ranch, so they were making plans to decorate the living room. They planned on about thirty people, so chairs had to be rented. Sheryl suggested a cupcake tree instead of the traditional tiered cake since they were having a limited number of guests.

Fresh flowers were hard to obtain in winter; however, the local florist promised to have enough for a two vases plus the bride's bouquet. He thought he could get roses.

Abby got crepe paper to make garlands and streamers to decorate the room. Agnes planned the menu to be served buffet style.

Agnes asked both girls to be her maids of honor, and Lay asked Doug to be his best man. He called on Witt to ask him to be in the wedding party.

"I'm not going to ask what happened between you and my daughter, but apparently, the both of you are going to be living in this neighborhood for some time. You can't hide for the rest of your life because, sooner or later, you are going to run into her. You might even have to speak to her. It probably would be easier for the both of you if you did it with people around and at a time she is too busy with her wedding duties to spend much time around you." Lay tried to reason with him.

"What you say is true. I'm not trying to hide, but it's just that it's too soon. I need a little more time. I'm trying to work through some things, and when I do, I'll be all right. I'm sorry, but you need to find someone else. Why don't you ask Tyler Tracy? It seems to me he would be the perfect man for the job." Witt refused Lay's request.

"Why on earth would I ask Tyler Tracy?" Lay didn't understand.

"Ask Abby. I'm sure she could tell you," Witt sadly answered. "Now, if you will excuse me, I have someone waiting for me. I wish only the best for you and Agnes. I hope you have a long, happy life together."

"Thank you for that. I'm trying to understand why you can't be there, but we will still miss you at the wedding. You come over any-time you can. I miss your smiling face." Lay shook hands with Witt as he left to return home.

'Ask Abby, I'm sure she could tell you.' Those eight words kept running through his mind. What could he possibly have meant? How was Tyler Tracy involved in this mess? As far as he knew, Abby hadn't even seen the boy since she moved back home. He could ask her, but that would be meddling. He still had faith that the two of them would eventually work things out and get back together.

The weather was perfect as the day of the wedding dawned on one of the rare warm days in February. The food was prepared, the rental chairs in place, the room decorated, and the wedding party was progressing as the guests began to arrive.

Sheryl helped her mother into her wedding dress. It had a fitted bodice styled with a modest V neckline and a short stand-up pleated collar at the nape with long tapered sleeves and a slightly flared skirt reaching halfway to her ankles. Abby covered the dress with a full-length sleeveless overlay of delicate lace in a slightly lighter shade of the soft orchid she used in the silk fabric of the dress. Abby had used some of the leftover lace and silk to fashion a small pillbox-style hat with a veil covering the upper half of her face. A pair of two-inch heels dyed the same shade as the dress completed the outfit. The diamond-and-opal necklace Lay had given to Agnes as a wedding gift was nestled perfectly within the neckline of the dress.

After a touching ceremony and a brief self-conscious kiss by the bride and groom, the festivities began. Once the toasts to the happy couple were made and they had their first dance, the floor was quickly filled with other happy dancers. A winter party was so rare that everyone wanted to make the most of the celebration.

It was well after midnight before the party broke up. People were reluctant to leave, but most of them had ranch chores to do early the next morning.

After everyone had gone, Abby and Sheryl put the food away and decided to leave the rest until morning. It had been a long day, and they were tired. Tomorrow was also going to be a busy day. Doug had to have Lay and Agnes at the airport in Denver for a ten thirty flight in the morning. That meant leaving home well before seven o'clock.

The bags were already packed and stacked in the spare room; all the reservations had been confirmed for their two-week honeymoon in Hawaii.

After seeing the happy couple off, the girls set about getting the house back in order. The chairs were wiped off and stacked on the porch, ready to be returned by Doug to the rental place later that afternoon. They decided to freeze the remainder of the cupcakes so Lay and Agnes could have them for later. The remaining food would be used as leftovers. Tablecloths and napkins had to be laundered and put away, the furniture put back to where it belonged, and the folding tables and chairs stored away.

By that evening, everything was in its proper place, wiping out all traces of the wedding. The house was strangely quiet without Lay and Agnes.

Everyone was relieved to get back to their normal routine the next day. Abby had a new client coming in, and Sheryl needed to get caught up on some of the bookwork she got behind on because of the wedding.

CHAPTER EIGHT

$\mathcal{T}$he newlyweds returned looking tanned and well rested after their two weeks of sitting on their private beach in front of the cabin they had rented. They couldn't wait to get to work, deciding on the final plans for their new house.

Lay rarely concerned himself with work on the ranch, only making an appearance when Doug wanted his advice or needed him to help out. He trusted Doug to handle the ranch business. Besides, he had more interesting things on his mind.

After seeing how happy his dad and Agnes were, Doug's thoughts began turning towards matrimony. He loved Sheryl with all of his being, and he was confident she returned his feelings. Why shouldn't they get married? First he had to come up with a plan. It had to be romantic. Maybe if they went to Duggin's… He had gone to school with Robert, the manager there. Perhaps together they could come up with something special. Champagne or maybe a violin player? Or a small combo? What was her favorite song? He knew she loved roses, so maybe he could use flowers. After a conversation with Robert at the restaurant, he had a plan—well, sort of one.

He was waiting for Sheryl to get home that evening to put things into motion.

"I never get you alone anymore," he complained, then suggested, "Why don't we get all dressed up Friday and go out to eat somewhere? Just the two of us."

"I would love that. Let's go to Duggin's. I really like their food." Sheryl liked the idea of just the two of them on a date. When she thought about it, they had been on very few dates by themselves; usually there were four of them.

Doug was pleased that Sheryl had picked the restaurant. That would add to her surprise.

On Tuesday, Doug went to the local flower shop to order a dozen roses. Six were to be delivered to By Design on Friday afternoon with a note that said: "I love you, and I owe you six more. You will be collecting them later." He was to pick up the remaining six from the florist on Friday afternoon.

Fifteen minutes before she was due home, he placed one rose on the bed in her room with a note attached that said: "I love you because you make me happy."

"Thank you for the flowers, but what's with the note?" Sheryl asked as soon as she arrived home and saw Doug. She was curious about where the other six roses were.

"Go get dressed, and maybe we can find out together," Doug answered cryptically.

"I'll hurry!" She turned and took the stairs two steps at a time.

By the time she returned downstairs, transformed into a vision of loveliness, carrying the first rose, Doug was dressed and had the car warmed and ready to go.

As Doug helped her in, on the car seat, she found a second rose with another note attached. "I love you because you make me feel like nothing is impossible when I'm with you."

"What are you up to, Doug?" she asked curiously.

"Just trying to have a night out with my best girl." He smiled as he answered.

"This is wonderful! We haven't been out alone nearly enough," Sheryl agreed.

"I think it's high time. It seems like there's always been four of us," Doug mused.

"I miss that foursome. I really wish we could do something about that. They need to be together." Sheryl was worried about her friend.

"I know. There's a piece missing in that puzzle, but neither of them will talk about it. I'll keep after Witt, and you keep an ear open in case Abby lets something slip." Doug turned into Duggin's parking lot. "Enough about them. This is our evening."

"That's fine with me." Sheryl allowed Doug to help her out of the car.

"Bring your roses in. I'll see if they'll put them in some water until we're ready to go home."

They were greeted at the door by Robert, who was holding a third rose with another note. It said: "I love you because you make me want to be a better person." He handed it to Sheryl and led the couple to a secluded table. There, another rose had been placed across her plate at the table with still another note. "I love you because you give me hope for the future."

Robert returned to the table with a vase for the four roses she had received.

'What are you up to, Douglas Andrews?' Sheryl was thoroughly enjoying the suspense and her night alone with Doug.

"Well, the first thing I think we should do is eat. Then we'll see where the evening takes us." Doug smiled at her as he signaled the waiter to begin serving their meal.

"But we haven't ordered." Sheryl was waiting for the menu.

"I already took care of that," he answered.

"How did you know what I wanted?" Sheryl asked.

"What's your favorite meal here?" he asked.

"Prime rib, scalloped potatoes, grilled asparagus, and a green salad," Sheryl replied. At that moment, her meal was placed in front of her, reflecting exactly what she had just said. "But how did you know?"

"I pay attention to details," he answered smugly. "Now, let's eat. I'm famished!"

After a wonderful meal, the waiter brought champagne and two glasses to the table along with another rose. Its note read: "I love you because I am nothing without you."

"Doug! What are you doing?" Sheryl asked as Doug stood, moved to stand in front of her, and dropped to one knee.

"I love you more than life itself, Sheryl Barry. Will you please do me the honor of becoming my wife?" Doug asked the big question.

"Douglas Andrews, I love you, and yes, I will marry you." Sheryl was nearly speechless, but she had no trouble answering his question.

As soon as she said yes, Robert handed her the last rose. With it was another note. "I love you. I don't think I could survive without you, so please don't ever change." Dangling from it, on a ribbon was her engagement ring. Doug removed the ring and placed it on her finger. Sheryl slipped out of her chair to join him on her knees for their first embrace as an engaged couple.

"Now you have your dozen roses," Doug whispered in her ear.

"And now I have you forever. Thank you," Sheryl whispered back as they stood for a second embrace and a tender kiss.

Everyone in the restaurant applauded.

Sheryl was so happy she didn't know whether to cry or laugh.

"Please allow me to be the first to congratulate you." Robert poured champagne for the couple and silently disappeared, leaving them to celebrate alone.

After the waiter had cleared his throat for the second time, they realized it was time for the restaurant to close. After apologizing, they made their way out to the car, carrying the vase with her six roses. Neither of them was anxious to rejoin the real world.

It was after midnight by the time they arrived home. Neither of them wanted to share their secret just yet, so they kissed good night and quietly went to their rooms after placing the last six roses in the vase with the first six.

***

The next morning, at breakfast, they shared their news with everyone. Lay and Agnes were overjoyed for them. Abby congratulated them, but it was all she could do not to burst into tears. She was happy for them but couldn't help but feel a little sorry for herself.

"Have you set the date yet?" Abby asked, trying her best to be enthusiastic.

"Not yet. Actually, I guess we haven't had time to think about it," Sheryl answered.

"It can't be too soon for me." Doug didn't want to wait.

"We'll have to talk about it," Sheryl answered even though she echoed his feelings.

Sheryl knew their news had to have hit Abby hard, but she covered well. After they arrived at the store, she hesitated to broach the subject, but she really wanted Abby to make her wedding dress. Abby hadn't said anything, but Sheryl knew it had to have been a little difficult for her to make her mother's wedding dress, and she was sure this dress would be a lot more wearing on her nerves. Darn that Witt! What was wrong with that man?

Abby was sure Sheryl would want her to make the wedding dress. She also knew Sheryl would hesitate to ask her because she would be afraid of upsetting her.

"If you'll let me, I would be happy to make your dress as a wedding gift to you and Doug," Abby offered before Sheryl could get up her nerve to bring the subject up.

"Oh, Abby. You are sure you won't mind? I mean, with what's happened between you and Witt? I really wanted you to, but I was afraid it might be too difficult for you." Sheryl was so relieved to have Abby make the offer.

"What happened to Witt and me is in the past. It's time for me to move on, and I can't think of a better way to do it than make your wedding gown." Abby put aside her feelings and held her tears until a time when she could be alone and agreed to make the dress.

Sheryl ran to the bookstore to get all the bride magazines she could find. The rest of the week, she spent every free moment poring over them, looking at all the styles. She couldn't decide what style she wanted, so she was hoping to combine parts of several of the dresses so Abby could create the perfect gown for her perfect day.

Finally, with the help of Sheryl's suggestions, Abby came up with a dress design that pleased Sheryl. As soon as she picked out the fabrics she wanted, Abby put in an order for them. While she was waiting on the fabric, she would make the pattern.

That night, Abby cried herself to sleep. She couldn't help it. She was still trying to say good-bye to her lost love and any wedding plans she had been harboring in her dreams. It would be so much easier if she only knew what she had done to make him hate her so.

One day, Katherine came in the store, looking for another dress to wear to a bridal shower to be given for Jennifer. She had looked at the ready-made dresses when she had been there earlier and remembered seeing one she liked. It was still there, so she purchased it.

While Sheryl was taking her money, Abby happened to see Witt's pickup in front of the store. He paused for a moment and then sped off. As she was wondering about his hesitation, another wave of sadness rolled over her. Why couldn't she get over him? He had quite obviously moved on.

After much discussion, Doug and Sheryl set their wedding date for June 20th.

Lay and Agnes planned to move into their new house by June 1st, so Lay would be free to run the ranch while Doug and Sheryl were on their honeymoon.

The first time Doug went to Denver, he stopped by a travel agency to pick up brochures. Agnes still had the ones they picked up earlier, but they were mostly for tropical vacations. The younger couple was more interested in going somewhere on a cruise.

Doug and Sheryl decided to have their wedding on the patio in the backyard. If it rained, they could put up the canopy. Either way, it would be a beautiful ceremony with family and friends attending.

The only flies in the ointment were Witt and Abby.

Doug and Sheryl desperately wanted them both to take part in the ceremony. The way things stood now, there was a strong possibility that neither of them would even be there.

Sheryl knew it was taking everything Abby had to make her wedding dress. She wanted so much to ask her to be her maid of honor. But so far, she hadn't worked up the courage to do that. The girl was on the edge now. She was afraid that being a member of the wedding party might be too much for her to handle. What was she going to do?

Doug was facing a similar problem with Witt. He didn't want anyone but Witt as his best man, but how was that going to happen with the way things were? Something had to be done.

"What are we going to do about Abby and Witt?" Doug asked Sheryl.

"We've got to get them back together," Sheryl answered.

"That's going to be easier said than done." Doug was out of ideas as to how to do that.

"You go try to talk to Witt again, and I will see what I can do with Abby." Sheryl sighed, not very hopeful that anything would come of it.

"Witt's coming over tomorrow. I'll give it another try. I guess we have nothing to lose." Doug prayed he could reason with Witt and talk some sense into his best friend.

"Do you remember that pact we made some years back to be each other's Best Man?" Doug opened the conversation with Witt while they were sitting on Doug's front porch.

"I remember," Witt answered after a short silence, his voice barely audible.

Doug jumped right in. "Sheryl and I are getting married on June 20th. I will need you front and center then."

"Sorry. I won't be able to do that." Witt sighed sadly as he turned his friend down.

"If you are going to let me down, don't you think I at least deserve an explanation?" Doug asked, hoping he might finally get something out of Witt.

"I guess I do owe you something." Witt paused, took a deep breath, let out another deep sigh, and then began, "All through high school, I took a backseat to Tyler Tracy with Abby. When he got engaged last year, I thought it was going to be my time at last, but she left town before I had a chance to see. Then when you started seeing Sheryl, I tagged along just so I could spend time with her. She seemed happy to be with me, so I got my hopes up."

"When your dad had his heart attack, and she moved back to town for a while, I was so happy because it meant I would get to spend more time her. Then the first thing I knew, Tracy was not engaged, and she was seeing him. Once again, I had to take a backseat. Then Tracy got engaged again. Before I even got a chance to ask her out, she was sneaking around to be with him. When she got caught, I was happy to help her out because I thought she would finally be done with him. When she went back to Centerview, I tagged along with you again just so I could, once more, spend some time with her. Every time I got to be with her, I thought I was making some headway. I thought we were getting closer. When she went back east, I loved the time I got to spend with her. She seemed to really enjoy being with me. I was beginning to believe we had a future."

Witt was up, pacing the floor, remembering. "And then, when she turned down that job at that fashion house in New York City, I had no doubt she had feelings for me. I began to plan a future for us. I was so happy when she moved back here and opened that store. We were getting closer every day. I was so in love with her that I began thinking of how I was going to propose to her. I was planning our whole future together." He had a sad half smile as he thought about that happier time. "The store hadn't been open a week when she started up with Tracy again. I cannot take a backseat one more time. I just can't. I'm finished with her. I don't think I can stand to be in the same room with her right now. Maybe someday. But not yet." He finished his explanation. "I'm sorry to let you down, Doug. But I just can't do it."

"As far as I know, she hasn't even seen Tracy since she's been back." Doug was sure he would have heard about it. "Sheryl would have told me."

"Then Sheryl's committing the sin of omission by not telling you! She was there! She has to know about it! She's just covering for Abby!" Witt lashed out.

"Are you absolutely sure about this?" Doug couldn't believe what Witt was saying.

"I saw him park his car right in front of the store, get out, and go in. I've seen his car parked in front of the store at least a half dozen times since then. He was there a week ago. I saw his car parked right out in front where it always is," Witt quietly answered.

"I can't believe that." Doug was shocked.

"Ask Sheryl. See if she will tell you the truth now. She has to be in on it! I know what I saw! You'll never convince me I didn't see him go into that store. I've got to go. I'll talk to you later." He left Doug sitting alone, completely at a loss as to what to think. He had to talk to Sheryl as soon as possible.

"I have to ask you a question, and I really need the absolute truth from you." Doug spoke with Sheryl the first time he got her alone.

"Of course, I'll tell you the truth. I always do. You should know that." Sheryl wondered what Doug was getting to.

"I do know that, but I had a very disturbing conversation with Witt today." Doug trusted Sheryl to always be truthful, but he was still upset about what Witt had told him.

"Was it about what's going on with him and Abby?" Sheryl asked.

"Yes." He took a deep breath and asked the question, "Has Abby been seeing Tyler Tracy since she's moved back here?"

"No. He came in the store just once right after we opened." Sheryl wondered where that question came from. "But it was to apologize to her again. She didn't want to be alone with him, so she asked me to stay, and I heard everything that was said. All he did was apologize to her and leave. He wasn't there more than fifteen minutes. She hasn't seen him since then, Doug. I swear that's the absolute truth."

"Witt believes they are having an affair, and it's killing him," Doug explained. "He claims he saw Tracy go in the store once and has seen his car parked in front of it a half dozen other times. He said the last time he saw his car there was last week."

"I swear to you he hasn't been in the store but that one time. When would she have time to have an affair? I'm with her all day, and she never goes anywhere by herself at night. Tyler is getting married in May. Why would he want to have an affair anyway?" Sheryl didn't understand.

"If you remember, he tried to have an affair with Abby once before while he was engaged," Doug reminded her.

"Oh, I forgot about that. What are we going to do?" Sheryl asked.

"I don't know. He really believes Abby is seeing Tracy again. We have to get them together so they can talk it out. If we don't do something, that's not going to happen any time soon."

"I'll talk to Abby again." Sheryl was going to try once more.

"Don't say anything to her just yet. We need to form a plan first," Doug cautioned her. "Let me try to talk to Witt again."

"You've got to convince him he's wrong. It can't end this way. It's all some kind of a terrible misunderstanding. It's up to us to fix this," Sheryl pleaded with him.

"I'm beginning to think this might be one of those things we may not be able to put back together no matter how hard we try." Doug tried to prepare Sheryl in case that happened.

"It can't end like this! I won't let it!" Sheryl wasn't about give up on their friends.

Doug went to see Witt the next day to relay to him what Sheryl had told him.

"I talked to Sheryl last night," he began. "She says Tracy was at the store one time right after they opened. Katherine came into the store one day, and while she was there, she asked Abby if she would allow Tracy to come in and apologize to her again. Abby left the door to her workroom open all the time he was there, so Sheryl could hear their entire conversation. All he did was apologize and leave. He wasn't there more than fifteen minutes. She swears that is the only time he has been in the store and the only time Abby has seen him. I believe her."

"I know what I saw. How do you explain that away?" Witt wasn't about to change his mind.

"I don't know, but I believe Sheryl. Would you talk to her?" Doug asked.

"Does Abby know about our conversation?" Witt asked.

"No. I haven't said anything, and I asked Sheryl not to," Doug assured him. "No one else knows anything about this."

"I don't know what good it will do, but I will listen to what she has to say," he agreed.

"I will bring her over tonight. We have to get this figured out before it goes any further." Doug hoped Sheryl could get through to Witt. Nothing else had helped the situation.

That evening, Doug and Sheryl found Witt waiting for them on the front porch of his house.

"Hello, Sheryl. It's good to see you. Congratulations on your engagement. I wish you and Doug many years of happiness," he greeted her.

"Thank you, Witt. But that isn't why I'm here. This thing with you and Abby has got to be figured out. Tyler was in the store once about a week after we opened. I was there and heard everything he said. He is in some kind of therapy and felt like he needed to apologize to her again for the way he had treated her. He came in, apologized, and left. He wasn't there more than fifteen minutes. I swear to you he has not been back to the store, and Abby has had no other contact with him, nor does she want any." Sheryl waited to see Witt's reaction.

"I saw him park his car in front of the store, get out, and go in. I have seen that same gray car parked right in front of the store at least a half dozen times. The last time I saw it there was a week ago. How do you explain that?" Witt still didn't believe what she was saying.

"Could it be another car that looks like his?" Sheryl wondered.

"No, it was the same car. I'm sure of it." Witt knew what he had seen.

"I know Tyler has never been in the store but that one time." Sheryl was equally positive.

"There's something wrong here. We've got to get this straightened out. Would you agree to talk with Abby? Maybe she has an explanation." Doug could make no sense out of it.

"I can't stand to see her just yet. Maybe later." Witt still couldn't bear to face Abby.

"Wait! Wait! Wait! Tyler doesn't have a gray car!" Sheryl exclaimed.

"You're right! His car is black!" Doug agreed with her.

"His mother's is gray though. I just remembered. The day he came in, he mentioned that he had to borrow her car because his was in the garage. Katherine came into the store and asked Abby to make her a dress for Tyler's wedding. She was there several times for fittings, and last week she came in and bought one of our ready-made dresses," Sheryl explained what probably happened. "That's it! You were watching the wrong car! That's all it was!"

"It can't be." Witt sank back in his chair.

"It is." Doug was satisfied they had finally figured it out.

"You jumped to the wrong conclusion and just about broke her heart. What are you going to do about it, Witt?" Sheryl demanded.

"If she will ever speak to me again, I'm going to spend the rest of my life trying to make it up to her. I don't know how I could have been so wrong about things. I should have had more faith in her." Witt sat with head in hands, totally defeated.

"Yes, you certainly should have trusted her. You could have, at the very least, talked to her and got her side of whatever you thought was going on. It would have avoided a lot of heartache on both sides. All you had to do was ask, Witt. Why didn't you?" Sheryl was really angry at Witt for all the trouble he had caused by not trusting Abby.

"What was I thinking, treating her like I did? I can't blame her if she never speaks to me again. I deserve anything she does to me." Witt was at a loss as to how to even begin to make things right with her. The way he had treated Abby was unforgivable.

"You had better come up with one humdinger of an apology. That's all I can say." If she hadn't been so angry at Witt, Sheryl would have felt sorry for him.

"It had better be a good one. If I were you, I would practice my groveling." Doug was so relieved to have figured everything out that he couldn't be upset with anyone.

"I don't know how to even start to apologize. I don't suppose either of you would have any suggestions?" Witt looked at Doug and Sheryl hopefully.

"Let me talk to Abby before you try to. Maybe I can soften her up a little," Sheryl offered to try to help—not so much to pave the way for Witt but to help her friend.

The next morning, Sheryl approached Abby, unsure how to start the conversation. "Doug and I had a long talk with Witt last evening. I think we've figured out what happened. It was all one gigantic misunderstanding. Witt would like very much to come and talk with you to try to explain, if you will give him a chance," Sheryl explained.

"So it was a misunderstanding, huh? Well, he didn't have enough faith in me to come and talk to me about what was bothering him then, so why would I trust anything he is going to say to me now?" Abby sadly refused. "How do I know he won't do the same thing again the next time he thinks I've done something wrong? No. I don't want to see or talk to him again. It's all over between us. Now I have work to do." She turned back to the sewing she had been busy with, thus ending the conversation.

Sheryl knew she would get nothing more from Abby today, so maybe Doug could get her to change her mind tonight.

"I did my best to persuade Abby to see Witt." Sheryl told Doug about their conversation that morning. "She doesn't want to see or talk to him. What are we going to do now?"

"I'll try to talk to her in a little while. Maybe I can get her to change her mind." Doug didn't have much hope, but he had to try. "He should have asked her about Tracy. He handled it all wrong, and I don't blame her one little bit for being upset with him."

"I spoke with Witt yesterday." Doug approached Abby the first chance he got. "He knows he made the biggest mistake of his life. He wants to try to explain if you will give him a chance to talk to you."

"He's had plenty of time to explain. Apparently, he chose not to, so it's too late now. I'm trying to forget what we had or what I thought we had. As I told Sheryl, I don't wish to see or talk to him. But I'm sure you already know that. I remember how the four of us used to be a team." Abby quietly gave her answer.

"It could be that way again if you would let it," Doug suggested.

"I'm sorry, but it's over. I wish it were different, but the fact is, it's not." Abby slowly walked up the stairs to her bedroom, closed the door, and let the pent-up tears flow. As much as she wanted to know why Witt stopped coming around, her pride wouldn't let her ask.

"Did you have any luck?" Sheryl asked as soon as she saw Doug.

"No. She's dug in her heels. She is not going to give in anytime soon," Doug answered.

"We are going to have to get them together somewhere so they can talk this thing out, and that's not going to be easy to accomplish," Sheryl suggested

"Wherever it is, there had better not be a back door," Doug asserted.

"There better not even be a window. She's pretty mad. I guess we could always lock them in her bedroom. If she had to look him in the eye, she might listen to what he has to say. Do you suppose we could stash Witt in there and, when she goes in, lock the door?" Sheryl asked, half in jest.

"We may have to if we can't come up with something else—and soon." Doug was beginning to think that probably was what they would end up having to do.

"Any other ideas?" Doug asked as soon as she got home the next evening.

"Not yet. When I went into Abby's workroom this morning, I could swear she had been crying. She wouldn't look at me, and I saw a damp tissue on her table. I'm sure she still loves him, but her pride is keeping her from admitting it," Sheryl answered.

"Okay, this has gone on long enough. I'll have Witt in her room before you get home tomorrow. You get her into that room as soon as you can." Doug had waited as long as he was going to. "We're going to lock the door and keep them in there together until she either forgives him or does him in."

"Right now, it could go either way," Sheryl added drily.

"I know. That's what I'm worried about. What if it doesn't work?" Doug had his doubts.

"It will. It just has to!" Sheryl was desperate.

***

Abby was shocked to see Witt sitting in her bedroom. Before she could turn around to make her escape, she heard the lock click on the door and knew there would be no way out. She knew Doug and Sheryl would be waiting on the other side of the door for as long as it took.

"Abby, I am so sorry to spring this on you like this, but I had to talk to you and try to explain what happened. But now that I'm here, I really don't quite know how to begin." Witt apologized for his presence there.

"Please, Witt. There's nothing you can say that will erase how you've made me feel the last few months." Abby moved to stand in front of the window, keeping her back to Witt. She didn't want him to see the tears threatening to spill out of her eyes. How was she going to get through this without falling apart? What were they thinking, locking her in her room with Witt? How could they be so cruel?

"You can't say anything to me that I haven't said to myself. I let you down by not trusting you. If only I had asked you what was going on instead of letting all those crazy thoughts get the best of me," Witt continued.

"Do you have any idea how you made me feel? You just quit coming around, and I had no idea why. I thought I would go crazy trying to figure out what I did to cause you to hate me so." She could say no more because she was choked up with the tears she could no longer hold back.

"No! Don't touch me!" She exclaimed when she heard the floor creak as he got up out of his chair and took a step toward her. As much as she longed to feel his arms around her again, she couldn't bear to have him touch her right now.

"It's killing me to know how much I've hurt you, and now you won't let me try to do something to make it better!" He wasn't far from tears himself. "What can I possibly do to make this up to you?"

"I'm not so sure there is anything you can do to fix what's wrong with us because I don't think I will ever get over what you have put me through. I doubt that I will ever be able to fully trust anyone again the way I trusted you, Witt." This whole conversation felt surreal. She could hear someone talking, but it couldn't be her. She was going to wake up from this dream any minute and return to the reality of the overwhelming sadness she had come to accept as her life.

By now they were both in tears—she for the loss of a soul mate and a life she could never have with him and he for the regret of having caused the only girl he had ever loved so much immeasurable pain.

"Abby, we have to get around this somehow. We can't let my stupid pride ruin what we had together. You are the only girl I have ever or will ever love. I'll spend the rest of my days trying to make this up to you if you will only give me the chance," Witt pleaded with her. If he thought it would help, he would gladly get on his knees.

"I can't deny that I still love you, but I just don't know if I can ever forgive you," she quietly admitted.

"Can't we just erase the past and start over again?" He was desperate. He couldn't lose her now that he knew she still loved him.

"Would you tell me one thing?" She turned from the window to face him for the first time.

"Anything." At least she was willing to listen to something.

"What did I do that caused you to stop loving me and take away the very best friend I have ever had?" Her voice was so low, he barely heard the words.

"Nothing! You did absolutely nothing! It was all me and my pride. Please sit down, and I will tell you the whole story." He knew it was time for absolute honesty.

***

Meanwhile, Doug and Sheryl were nervously waiting on a bench just outside that locked bedroom door.

Lay, wondering where everyone was, climbed the stairs in search of them.

"Why are you two sitting way up here?" he asked.

"We have Witt and Abby locked in her room," Doug admitted.

"I would call that meddling. We don't usually do that around here," Lay commented.

"We had to do something. Nothing we had tried before was working, and they sure weren't going to make up on their own," Doug explained.

"Once we found out what the problem was, we knew we had to do what we could to get things straightened out between them," Sheryl added.

"You got them to talk about their personal life?" Lay asked.

"Not hers, his. He thought she had taken up with Tracy again, and he was so in love with her that it was killing him. He couldn't face her knowing once again she had chosen Tracy over him. The only thing he could think to do was cut her out of his life and do his best to get over her," Doug filled Lay in.

"But that certainly wasn't working out for him. He was utterly miserable," Sheryl added.

"And you figured all this out how?" Lay was a little curious.

"Witt turned me down when I asked him to be my best man, so I told him I thought he owed me an explanation, and miracles of miracles, he spilled the whole story," Doug explained. "It turns out to be one colossal misunderstanding."

"But then she refused to even talk to him so they could get things sorted out. This is the best plan we could come up with. We were desperate." Sheryl hoped Lay would understand.

"You must have been to dream this up. How long have they been in there?" Lay asked.

"Almost an hour." Sheryl looked at her watch.

"That's quite a while. Do you think they're all right?" Lay couldn't help but wonder.

"We can still hear Witt's voice, so she hasn't killed him yet," Doug answered.

"Is that a possibility?" Lay grinned as he asked the question.

"She's pretty mad at him." Sheryl returned his grin.

"Well, move over, and I'll wait with you." Lay joined them on the bench.

***

"That is the whole story," Witt finished his confession. "I once read somewhere that people in love sometimes do stupid things. I'm living proof that it is an absolutely true statement. I jumped to a conclusion and didn't make an effort to get the facts before I took action. My biggest mistake though was not having enough faith in you. I am so very sorry for that." He sat quietly, head bowed, waiting for a response from her.

"Tyler was foremost in my thoughts for more years than he deserved to be. When I think about it, I used you all through those years—not intentionally, but I did. For that, I am truly sorry. Tyler killed any feelings I may have had for him when he took me to that motel. I didn't tell you that, so you had no way of knowing. That was a mistake on my part. I should have told you. All I would have had to do was ask you what was going on when you quit coming around. I didn't do that. That was another mistake on my part. I should have asked." Abby had a lot of thinking to do before she would be able to get things straight in her own mind. Until she did that, she knew she couldn't truly begin the process of attempting to put the whole episode behind her.

"When I saw Tracy go into your store, it was like somebody punched me in the stomach. I couldn't breathe. Then when I started seeing what I assumed to be his car parked out in front of your store so many times, it nearly destroyed me. As far as I knew, you still had feelings for him, and I was once again going to have to take a back-seat to Tyler Tracy. It just about broke my heart. Even so, I couldn't help myself. I drove past your store as often as I could just to try to get a glimpse of you, but I couldn't bring myself to face you." Witt wasn't really sure exactly why he didn't talk to her except that he was so certain there could be no other explanation. "I might have been able to cut you out of my life eventually, but I could never get you out of my heart. No matter how hard I may try not to be, I will always be hopelessly in love with you, Abby." After a long silence, Witt dared ask, "So how do we move on from here?"

"I don't know. We can't go on as if nothing happened." Abby thought she was beginning to understand how the whole thing might have come about, but she also knew she wasn't going to be able to just forget the pain his actions had caused her.

"All I'm asking is that you give me a second chance. However long it takes, I'll follow any rules you lay down and do anything you ask of me." Witt was beginning to hope there might be a chance for them yet. She was at least listening to what he had to say.

"It's going to take me some time to work through everything. I honestly don't know if I can get past all of it." She wondered if they would even be able to start over. "You're going to have to earn my trust. Until then, I may still have my doubts about everything you do. I'm sorry, but that's the way I feel. I can't help it."

She truly wanted to try to trust Witt again. She had missed spending time with him and having long talks with him about everything and nothing. Oh, how she wanted to feel his arms around her again. She missed listening to Doug and him as they teased each other. She wanted the four of them to be friends again and spend time together as they once did. She wanted her old life back. But could it ever be the same after this? She knew she had to, at the very least, make an effort to find out.

"Maybe we can go back to just being friends at least for a while. Do you think you could live with that? No romance. Just friendship," she asked thoughtfully.

"It would be so wonderful to have you back as a friend, Abby. I think I've missed our conversations most of all. If you will allow me to spend time with you, then I'll wait as long as it takes. You set the pace." Witt gladly accepted her stipulations.

Abby walked across the room and knocked on the door. "You can let us out now." She had no doubt Doug and Sheryl would be waiting just outside.

Instantly, the door was opened.

"Did you get everything worked out?" Sheryl was the first to speak.

"No. But I think maybe we will in time," Abby answered quietly.

"You all go on downstairs. I'll be there in a few minutes." She stood by the door until Witt and the others started down the staircase, then turned and walked back across the room to stand at the window, looking up at Polly for a long moment.

Then she smiled broadly. "He still loves me, Polly. And I love him. Perhaps my dreams will come true after all."

***

What happened, Witt?" Doug asked as they were making their way down the stairs.

"I think I may have barely squeaked by. She is giving me another chance. We are going to try to start over—as friends." Witt let out a big sigh of relief.

"You better treat her right from now on. I doubt that we will be able to pull your fat out of the fire a second time," Doug warned him.

"You don't have to worry about that. From now on, I'm going to spend all day, every day, proving to her that she can trust me. I've got a second chance with the love of my life, and I'm not about to blow it." Witt swore to himself he would never let Abby down again. He was going to spend the rest of his life doing his best to make her happy, and above all, he would never ever doubt her again.

By the time Abby joined the others downstairs, Agnes had a snack fixed for them. The four friends took their tray out to the front porch and sat together, listening to the quiet of the Colorado evening as they had done many times before.

It had turned out to be a very good evening.

EPILOGUE

*D*oug and Sheryl had their beautiful wedding on the patio amid perfect spring weather. Lay very happily walked Sheryl down the aisle. Witt was best man and Abby the maid of honor.

It was four months before Witt and Abby shared their second 'first kiss', and they were married the next spring. Lay proudly walked his second daughter down the aisle; Doug was best man and a very pregnant Sheryl matron of honor.

Abby got her new house. She made sure Polly was visible from every bedroom so the majestic mountain peak could watch over the little family who would thrive there for many wonderful years.

Lay and Agnes moved into their new house and lived there very happily for many years, entertaining their grandchildren. Within two years, they were grandparents to Doug's two sons and Abby's little girl named Polly.

ABOUT THE AUTHOR

*J*oyce Armintrout was born in a farmhouse near the small town of Peculiar, Missouri.

She grew up in that same house and is very proud of her country background.

By the time she was ten, she was writing short essays about things that happened on the farm. By the eighth grade, she had become interested in cowboy subjects. Her favorite cowboys were Roy Rogers and Gene Autry.

She spent many happy hours riding her horse and dreaming up adventures to write about.

Shortly after entering high school, she discovered the romance novel, so her subject matter changed considerably. She turned to the teenage romances going on around her. Anytime there was a breakup, the couple involved were sure to become the subject of her next story.

She never outgrew her love for the romance subjects. Her characters became more mature and with different and more complex problems.

Her retirement from AT&T gave her more time to devote to her writing. She divides her time with writing about her life on the farm and other memory pieces about her childhood and short stories about life going on around her. That retirement also gave her the time to write romance novels.

This is her second book to be published.

CPSIA information can be obtained
at www.ICGtesting.com
Printed in the USA
FFOW04n0638121116
29186FF